"What?" Erica snapped at Phoebe.

"Look in the bench behind you nine o'clock," Phoebe whispered fiercely. "Tell me, isn't he fine? He looks like Boris Kodjoe, with that clean shaven head and neat moustache. Isn't he gorgeous?"

Erica sighed, she would give this so-called handsome specimen a look then she would tell off Phoebe. This was getting ridiculous.

She glanced around quickly, then had to swing her head round again. He was handsome, full lips straight nose. She could bet his eyelashes were long close up. He had on a black shirt and blue jeans pants and his legs looked like they were long. He also had a worried furrow between his eyes and he was looking on at the proceedings as if his mind was not quite on it.

"Didn't I tell you?" Phoebe was whispering fiercely in Erica's ear, "and to think all this time he was sitting right near us, and look, no ring on any of his fingers. Indeed God is good."

Erica swung around to look at him again and he looked at her at the same time. She was caught red handed, she felt herself getting warm under the scarf she had around her neck, like a naughty child being caught in the cookie jar.

LOVING MR. WRIGHT

BRENDA BARRETT

JAMAICA TREASURES

LOVING MR. WRIGHT
A Jamaica Treasures Book/December 2012

Published by Jamaica Treasures
Kingston, Jamaica

This is a work of fiction. Names, characters, places, and incidents are either the product of the author's imagination or are used fictitiously. Any resemblance to an actual person or persons, living or dead, events, or locales is entirely coincidental.

ISBN - 978-976-95486-7-1
Jamaica Treasures Ltd.
P.O. Box 482
Kingston 19
Jamaica W.I.
www.fiwibooks.com

ALSO BY BRENDA BARRETT

Di Taxi Ride and Other Stories
The Pull of Freedom
The Empty Hammock
New Beginnings
Full Circle
The Preacher And The Prostitute
Private Sins (Three Rivers)
Loving Mr. Wright (Three Rivers)
Unholy Matrimony (Three Rivers)
If It Ain't Broke (Three Rivers)
Homely Girl (The Bancrofts)
Saving Face (The Bancrofts)
Tattered Tiara (The Bancrofts)
Private Dancer (The Bancrofts)
Goodbye Lonely (The Bancrofts)
Practice Run (The Bancrofts)
Sense Of Rumor (The Bancrofts)
A Younger Man (The Bancrofts)
Just To See Her (The Bancrofts)
Going Solo (New Song)
Duet On Fire (New Song)
Tangled Chords (New Song)
Broken Harmony (New Song)
A Past Refrain (New Song)
Perfect Melody (New Song)
Love Triangle: Three Sides To The Story
Love Triangle: After The End
Love Triangle: On The Rebound

ABOUT THE AUTHOR

Books have always been a big part of life for Jamaican born Brenda Barrett, she reports that she gets withdrawal symptoms if she does not consume at least two books per week. That is all she can manage these days, as her days are filled with writing, a natural progression from her love of reading. Currently, Brenda has several novels on the market, she writes predominantly in the historical fiction, Christian fiction, comedy and romance genres.

Apart from writing fictional books, Brenda writes for her blogs blackhair101.com; where she gives hair care tips and fiwibooks.com, where she shares about her writing life.

You can connect with Brenda online at:
Brenda-Barrett.com
Twitter.com/AuthorWriterBB
Facebook.com/AuthorBrendaBarrett

Chapter One

Erica drove into the shrub lined driveway of her sister's former home and felt a surge of loneliness so palpable it hit her like a dull thud somewhere in the region of her heart. Her sister, Kelly, and her family were gone to the Cayman Islands to live and for now, she had volunteered as their house sitter.

It was a job she was happy to do because her apartment, though walking distance from where she worked as a hotel nurse, was really just a glorified studio, and she relished the prospect of living again in a real house with yard space. She glanced over at the lawn. It had just started to sprout some wayward patches of grass and already looked overgrown. A gentle breeze touched the greenery and the clumps of grass seemed to wave at her mockingly—*you cannot take care of a yard as big as this*, they seemed to say to her.

Erica sighed and parked in front of the garage. How would she putter around in a five bedroom, four-bathroom house with almost half an acre of yard space dedicated to flowers and exotic shrubs?

This was a family home. She picked some lint off her jeans. In the past, she was quite happy to visit her sister and lounge on her verandah sipping drinks or scrounging around in her kitchen for food.

Now, here she was, all alone: no children to play with and no sister to argue with. She felt a gaping hole that her sister and her family used to fill and for the first in a long time, she realized that she really had no life.

She worked at the hotel Flamingo as a nurse, where she dispensed painkillers and kept up with the light work. Her job now was a far cry from her duties in the surgical ward. It was now more laid back and less stressful.

That's all she did, work, hang out with her sister's children, occasionally have lunch with her mother, and go to church. She was happily living the life of a spinster, but she had no male prospect on the horizon to get excited about, and nobody to get excited about her.

She looked down at her size 14 jeans balefully. Lately she had been spending way too much time eating. The jeans she had on could barely fit her. She had struggled to get into them this morning and now she was shuddering to think of how she would get out of them.

"Pathetic!" Erica muttered impatiently, taking her box out of the car and heading into the house.

The house felt empty—even though there was furniture in it—as if it knew that the rightful owners were away. She had a plan to cart over a box or two of her belongings every day until she had fully moved in.

She headed toward the guest room at the very end of the hallway upstairs. She was used to staying in that room when she visited in the past and she always thought that it was cooler than the rest of the rooms in the house. It had a balcony, which had an unobstructed view of the town of Ocho Rios. She gazed out of the window for a while and then sat on the bed, staring into space.

Maybe she should call her sister and let her know that she was just starting the moving-in process, but then again, they had left just one week ago and she had spoken to Kelly at least twice per day—asking her questions about Cayman, hanging onto her every word. She really needed to get a life apart from her sister and her family. As the older sister, by four years, she had always thought that she would be the first to get married and have children, but here she was, still single and for the first time in a long time she felt the first stifling stirrings of unhappiness grip her heart; that feeling, that everybody in the world was happier than she was. She thought she had quenched these feelings a long time ago.

She grabbed her cell phone and punched in her mother's number. The two of them were unusually close for a mother and daughter, maybe because she had nobody else to hang out with. All her friends were married or had children and were too busy raising their families to care about her. Usually she was fine with that, but today she felt slightly down because of her situation.

The phone on her mother's end rang for a while and then a breathless Lola came on the line. "Erica, I thought you would have been down here."

"Where?" Erica frowned slightly. "What are you up to?"

"I'm at church," Lola said, "getting my heart checked, my blood pressure checked and doing an eye test."

"What for?" Erica asked puzzled.

"The medical professionals from church, are doing a free day," Lola said exasperatedly. "Were you not at church when it was announced? Shouldn't you be down here helping? Aren't you a medical professional?"

"Oh, I forgot all about it," Erica said sullenly. "I was just moving in."

"Aah," Lola said soothingly. "You are feeling a bit down."

"Yes," Erica mumbled. "I am missing Kelly and the children a tad bit more than I should. I suddenly feel as if I have no life."

"Do you know what a good remedy for that is?" Lola asked sweetly.

"What mother?" Erica asked suspiciously, "get married, and have my own babies?"

"Nooo…well yes," Lola laughed. "I was thinking that your present situation could be remedied if you come and help out down here. You don't have to go to the hotel until in the evening. Come on down and take your mind off your empty nest."

"Okay," Erica sighed, "might as well."

When she drove into the church parking lot she had her car's AC on full blast and was reluctant to get out of the car. For some reason this summer felt like the hottest on record. However, the full parking lot was an indication that the heat was not a deterrent to people attending the health fair. She could already see, from her vantage point, several white circular tents with signs on the white flaps announcing various medical procedures. The parking lot did not have enough space though and several tents were pitched on the church lawn.

Erica grimaced. Hyacinth Donahue was going to have a fit. Her precious heliconia flower leaves, which she maintained as a matter of pride, and which made for a very colorful hedge, were being used as temporary umbrellas and fans.

There were long lines in front of each tent, and persons were milling around with small packages in hand. She spotted a health food tent and vowed to check it out. Maybe it was time she started eating healthier. The thought made her gag a little, but enough was enough; she hadn't gotten this big because she was eating healthily.

She pushed her hands into her white overcoat; even the short sleeves felt hot.

"Sister Erica, so glad you are here." Dr. Mansoon grinned when he saw her. "You forgot about this, didn't you?"

"Yup," Erica nodded, grinning back at him. "I was talking to my mother on one of my routine calls to her and she reminded me."

"Well," Dr. Mansoon patted his shirt pocket and dragged out a badge with her name on it. "You are not the only one who is missing in action today. I have three more badges. We assigned you to the eye-care booth for routine eye tests—get to working Nurse." He gave her a mock scowl.

"It seems as if the whole town is here," Erica said taking the badge from him.

He grunted and then spun around when somebody shouted his name. "Got to go."

Erica nodded and made her way to the eye-care booth. It was routine work for her and slightly boring.

Her small booth was supposed to be manned by two nurses but when Sister Darcy saw her coming, she handed the clipboard to Erica and explained the routine. "When the nurse from this booth detects that something is seriously wrong, send them to that booth." She pointed to an adjoining booth. "Write your findings and the doctor over there will take it from there. Simple." She then gave Erica a smirk and said, "Gotta run…have things to do."

After the long line receded from her booth, and mercifully, the sun had receded behind an ominous looking cloud, Erica sat gazing over the parking lot. The community had really taken advantage of the church's initiative to provide free health care. It was something that the medical professionals at the church had wanted to do for a long time.

Erica could barely remember discussing this venture at the last meeting. At the time she was distracted by her sister's unfortunate situation.

She still couldn't believe that Kelly had been brave enough to have had an affair and then had her lover's baby. If she had a husband like Theo she would never, in a million years, have looked at someone else.

She always dreamed of marrying a man like Theo, a man who loves his woman with such a deep abiding love that nothing could shake it.

She exhaled. She was happy that Theo took back Kelly after her extra marital affair, but she still shuddered to think of the long term consequences that the affair would have on the family.

Maybe it was better for her to remain single and unattached than to go through the emotional wringer that relationships seem to offer. She had tried to be the perfect girlfriend to two men in the past, but both times she had to leave the relationship broken hearted.

*****

She had known Corey from high school and he had been her first love but he left her when she became a Christian. "Can't handle the rules," he told her sheepishly. "Christianity is a bag of rules and I am a free thinker."

She moped around for years after that, yearning for a stable Christian man to recognize that she was wife material. Then she met Jay-Jay: Jason Jolly.

He was handsome, had a good job and seemed God-fearing. He had proposed to her on a Tuesday night. She had just gotten off shift from her job at Three Rivers Bay Hospital and he had gone down on one knee.

The Wednesday morning his wife had called her, asking if bigamy was no longer illegal in Jamaica. Erica had been shocked. It had taken her the better part of her thirties, when she still had a semblance of a waist, to get over Jay-Jay.

Now here she was, single and lonely. The kind of loneliness that usually had a single woman of thirty-five—with no real prospects—feeling that she had to do something about her situation.

Obviously, Mr. Right was nowhere near her radius.

"Why are you frowning, Sister Erica?" Phoebe stood before her, smiling.

"Oh, hi Phoebe," Erica grinned at the younger girl. Phoebe was gorgeous, had smooth golden skin, long wavy black hair, perfect teeth, tall and shapely but for some strange reason the men of the church avoided her like the plague. Her beauty would draw them like a moth to the flame, but a few days in her presence and, one by one, they would slink away in fear.

Phoebe was the church pariah, and as Sister Freda would put it, "There was still justice in this world," because one by one unattractive single women were marrying while Phoebe remained curiously unattached.

Phoebe sat down across from Erica and looked at a folder. "The welfare division of the church is catering for this event and we would like your order. We have several vegetarian options, and fish."

"Fish," Erica said conclusively. "Don't need to hear the vegetarian dishes."

"Okay." Phoebe scribbled the information on paper.

"I heard that Sister Kelly and the children left last week."

Erica nodded. She was reluctant to talk about Kelly with

anybody at church, even if it was in answer to innocent queries.

"I think Pastor Palmer is a very good man for staying with her."

Erica shrugged. "It's their business."

Phoebe nodded. "True, but the church felt kind of cheated that they did not hear the whole story or that we couldn't have a say."

Erica widened her eyes. "Why should the church have a say in the lady's business?"

"What our pastor does is our business," Phoebe shrugged. "We were concerned."

"He is no longer your pastor," Erica scratched her chin, "no need for them to publicize their life to all and sundry."

"Well, what I really wanted to know…" Phoebe cleared her throat, "is Elder Chris over Kelly?"

Erica laughed. "Phoebe, you are something else."

Phoebe shrugged. "I knew you wouldn't tell me anything, but now that he is free, can I have a go at him?"

Erica couldn't contain herself. She got up from the chair and started to laugh so hard several people stopped to see what was so funny.

Phoebe calmly sat in front of her and watched Erica until she calmed down.

"You are a riot," Erica wheezed, wiping the tears from her eyes. "Didn't you stalk Chris for a whole month until he came to church and publicly asked you to leave him alone?"

Phoebe smiled. "He called it stalking. I called it checking him out."

Erica gave Phoebe an assessing look. "You need to let men do the chasing for a change, Phoebe. Just look at you, when you walk into a room women move closer to their men and men can't help looking at you with their mouths opened…

but here at Three Rivers you have such a bad reputation that the men have vowed to stay far from you. That is not normal. The pretty girl should be able to pick, choose, and refuse who she wants to be with. You are really an exception to that rule."

Phoebe twirled a strand of her hair. "I don't like just anybody. He has to be tall, handsome and rich. Did I say rich?"

Erica nodded. "You did."

"That's why I convinced Sister Freda to put a singles section in the church newsletter with a picture of the single person and their occupation. I wanted her to put their income but I guess you can't have it all."

Erica grunted, "Why are you so gung ho to get married? You are just twenty-three. I am thirty-five and I am not married. Do you see me going around moping about my singleness?"

"That's because you had Sister Kelly as distraction," Phoebe said smugly. "Now you are just like the rest of us—single, working at a job which you have a love/hate relationship with, sitting in church week after week, trying to convince yourself that being single is okay and that you don't want anybody and you are quite happy the way you are. When deep down," Phoebe grinned wickedly, "you fear that one morning you will wake up and look in the mirror and see white hairs popping up all over your head, your waist line has expanded, your child bearing years are over, and you are still lonely and single and poor."

Erica stared at Phoebe in horror. Well she had thought about that on more than one occasion, but not the poor part. She did not have Phoebe's unholy fascination with money, but the lonely and single part was spot on.

She was just in her thirties and that wasn't old. However,

which woman wouldn't think about being lonely while staring at the slippery slope of the big four oh.

Apart from that, the church brethren were notorious for shoving the —you need to settle down—spiel down her throat.

"Well I … I have thought about the fact that I have no real Christian prospects but, I would not even think of going outside the church to look for a spouse…too many things to contend with. I think life is easier when you have a man who fears God, don't you think?"

Phoebe nodded. "My point exactly. I could be married by now, but I am still holding on for a good Christian man who is not a womanizer, rich like Midas, and handsome as a Nubian prince."

Erica chuckled. "Maybe we should start a singles club, where we share our pain."

Phoebe sat up straighter. "Maybe we should, but that would do me no good. In case you don't realize, I am not the most loved person around here."

Erica grinned. "I wonder why."

"Stupid men get insecure when I ask them about their income and what their future prospects are for a promotion." Phoebe shook her head in disgust. "I have never understood why that is so offensive. Would they rather I act all coy and innocent? I don't want to know what their favorite color is or which movie they want to watch. I just want to know if I can have a comfortable future with them. Every woman wonders that, I am just outspoken about it," Phoebe said heatedly.

"All right, all right," Erica said, "take it easy."

"Anyway, enough about that. I was wondering," Phoebe, looked at Erica earnestly, "what are you doing tonight?"

"Well, I was planning on hauling two more boxes of my stuff to Kelly's and then watching re-runs of The Cosby

Show."

Phoebe sighed. "Sounds boring. I can think of something infinitely more interesting."

"What?" Erica asked curiously.

"We could go to Great Pond Church. They are having a musical evening with their all male chorale."

Erica snorted. "I am not groupie material, Phoebe. I am overweight, almost middle aged and too cynical."

Phoebe shrugged. "You are never going to find someone if you don't go visiting other churches. Besides, you are not that bad. You have blemish free skin," she squinted her eyes and looked at Erica contemplatively. "Your face is not that plain, you have an attractive dimple when you smile, and your eyes are slanted just a little at the sides to look a tad bit exotic."

Erica nodded. "Go on. I am liking this."

"Your uhm… your hair is thick and bouncy and curls along your ear attractively."

Erica laughed. "Curls along my ear, I can work with that."

"Your eyes are slightly blood shot but when clear they look intelligent and there is a smile lurking there. I think your body can use some serious work but that's just me, lots of men claim that they like full bodied women."

Erica groaned. "You were doing so well, until you started on my body."

"You are good-looking, okay," Phoebe said exasperated. "The things people have to say to get a drive to Great Pond. If I had a car I would not be complimenting you so long and hard."

Erica grinned. "Well you did a good job. I'll pick you up at six."

Phoebe got up hurriedly. "I've got to go take the orders for the other people. Okay, six it is. I'll be waiting out at my front gate, so try to come on time. I have a new neighbor who is trying to get my attention, but he is unemployed. Don't know why he even bothers to try."

Erica rolled her eyes. "Okay ma'am, six it is."

Chapter Two

Caleb jumped off the bus at Great Pond and rubbed his leg. The conductor had booted him through the door like yesterday's rubbish. He winced and brushed himself off. He was trying to explain to the young man that he had no money. He had walked all day from the Adult Remand Center and had seen the bus in Spanish Town and exhausted, he had tiredly sunk into a bus seat.

He had no money, no friends, and no family. His aunt Reba had died three years ago while he was in prison. Fortunately, she had the foresight to leave a will and she named him as her only heir, making him the owner of ten acres of farmland, a run down two-bedroom house, three goats, and a cow.

The harried legal aide had handed him the papers with a smile. "It is in St. Ann, a place called Three Rivers…a lovely side of the island. You will do fine."

The prison warden had shoved some papers at him to sign and he was practically shoved out of the gates of the correctional center with a black plastic bag containing his old jeans and an old blue shirt from five years ago when he was first arrested. The clothes smelled moldy and were stiff.

He had a mind to dump the plastic bag in the nearest garbage bin and sit outside the thick prison walls and howl, but the bag contained all his possessions. If the legal aide had not bought him the shoes, jeans, shirt, and new underwear, he would have had to wear the old smelly stiff clothes.

He grimaced and felt hopelessly lost; the feeling of freedom was overshadowed with apprehension and uncertainty. He had absolutely no idea where he was going. He knew where St. Ann was, and could vaguely recall taking a trip with his father to visit his grand aunt, Reba. His mother had long jumped ship when he was born and he only had his father for familial ties. Since his incarceration, his father had abandoned him completely and his remaining family members wanted nothing to do with him. No cousins or siblings came to visit. He was on his own.

He was brought back to the present when he felt a drop of rain on his arm. He looked up at the evening sky in despair, not even a star in sight; it was thickly overcast. He looked up the road into the distance and saw several cars parked at the side of the road at what looked like a church. He could even hear singing. Down the road he could barely make out the sign 'Welcome to Great Pond.'

He was of two minds: he could wonder around in the dark all night, having no idea where he was, or he could go to the church and sit at the back. Hopefully, no one would realize he was there. He patted his head; he had been clean-shaven just this morning by the prison barber, so he knew he looked decent. When he looked in the mirror this morning he had looked a far cry from the scruffy dreadlocked man he was used to glimpsing in the mirror on Sundays when they allowed the men out in the cramped auditorium for church—thanks to the barber he now had a neatly trimmed beard and moustache.

He had loved those times; it was a comfort to his soul because every day, for two long years, he had gotten up bitter and angry. He used to plot how he could easily kill the woman that had been instrumental in getting him behind bars, but then he had attended the weekly meetings that the various churches had every Sunday and slowly his anger subsided. He had begun to look forward to the singing and then he had accepted one of those blue New Testament Bibles and gradually read it through. Eventually he started talking to God regularly. He gave his life to Christ and was baptized by the prison chaplain. His cellmates had started calling him Jesus Boy and ribbed him about it day and night, but he didn't care.

He slowed his steps before he entered the foyer of the church. This would be his very first church visit, if the prison chapel were not counted.

He stepped into a very busy crowd of people who were in various choir robes. He glanced through the church doors and looked inside, it was partially full, but there were a couple of empty seats on the backbenches.

"Oh excuse me," a young lady with long braided hair said to him, her eyes bright, "do you have a program?"

He shook his head.

"How come?"

"Huh?" she asked puzzled. "Aren't you the MC?"

"Nooo," he said slowly.

"Oh sorry," she said flinging her braids around to her back and storming off.

He looked down at himself and half smiled. He was fresh out of prison and one girl had mistaken him for the Master of

Ceremonies. He wasn't such a stand out then. He inwardly sighed and went into the church. There were four rows of benches; the seats were wide and padded. He headed for the left, which seemed like the least conspicuous place to be.

He sat behind two women. One of them was impossibly pretty and he had to shake his head and look at her again. She had what looked like hip length wavy hair and the longest eye lashes he had ever seen on a woman. She was whispering to her full-bodied friend. He couldn't see her face properly but he heard her chuckling.

He contemplated moving but he wanted to look at the pretty girl some more. They both smelled nice and for a split-second, he realized that he had given up the bitter animosity that he had felt toward women and the vow he had made never to go near one again.

He found himself straining to hear them.

"They said they'd start at seven, Erica," the pretty one said to her friend. "How was I to know that this church has a time issue?"

Erica shrugged. "No sweat off my back, I would have been curled up in the settee watching a movie now and eating a tub of ice cream. This is actually not such a bad way to spend the evening."

The pretty one shrugged. "All the so-called men on the male chorale are boys. I cannot marry a boy. Boys are broke and are either at school, financing an education, or obsessed with cars and brand name shoes. I need a man to finance the life I am not accustomed to."

Caleb flinched when he heard that. *So, she was a gold digger.* He actually moved up higher on the bench, he didn't want to hear her friend's reply. She was probably a gold digger too.

A gold digger caused him to go to prison for five years. He

almost lost his life. He lost his family, and had no reputation to speak of. Because of that woman he didn't even know where he was going to sleep tonight. He closed his eyes tightly willing the memories to stay at bay. He kept his eyes closed until he heard the MC announcing the beginning of the program.

Chapter Three

The music was extremely good and Erica found herself rocking to more than one song and getting as excited as the rest of the crowd. The church was now packed to capacity and though there was a late start, they were having a good time. Phoebe whispered to Erica non-stop about who was good-looking, who was not, who looked like marriage material, and who was perennially single. Phoebe was a treasure trove of banal, shallow conversation and despite the lovely program Erica felt like shaking her.

"Oh my," Phoebe whispered in her ear once again.

Erica stiffened. She was just about to tell Phoebe to shut up once and for all. Not even her five and seven year old niece and nephew were so fidgety and talked so incessantly. It was like being out with a restless hormone driven teenager.

"What?" Erica snapped at Phoebe.

"Look in the bench behind you, nine o'clock," Phoebe whispered fiercely. "Tell me, isn't he fine? He looks like Boris

Kodjoe with that clean-shaven head and neat moustache. Isn't he gorgeous?"

Erica sighed. She would give this so-called handsome specimen a look, then she would tell off Phoebe—this was getting ridiculous.

She glanced around quickly, then, had to swing her head around again. He was handsome: full lips, straight nose. She could bet his eyelashes were long when seen close up. He had on a black shirt and blue jeans pants and his legs looked like they were long. He also had a worried furrow between his eyes and he was looking on at the proceedings as if his mind was not quite on it.

"Didn't I tell you?" Phoebe was whispering fiercely in Erica's ear. "And to think, all this time he was sitting close to us...and look, no ring on any of his fingers. Indeed God is good."

Erica swung around to look at him again and he looked at her at the same time. She was caught red handed. She felt herself getting warm under the scarf she had around her neck, like a naughty child being caught with her hand in a cookie jar.

He didn't smile at her or anything; he just stared with almost no expression on his handsome face. Another group was about to start singing and he didn't look on the stage, neither did she. It was now a competition to see who would win in the stare down.

Erica refused to look away first so she inspected him quietly. His eyes looked weary and tired and there was a slight slump to his shoulders. He endured her scrutiny and then raised an eyebrow.

Erica raised back her eyebrow.

He sighed and then broke the eye contact almost sullenly crossing his arms and leaning back on the bench; once again staring ahead.

"What was that about?" Phoebe whispered frantically. "He wasn't even looking at me. He was looking at you."

"It was war," Erica, said, smiling. "I think I like him."

"Oh, no you don't," Phoebe said. "I saw him first."

Erica grinned. "He looks mysterious, kind of dangerous, don't you think?"

Phoebe cleared her throat. "Well, he does look a bit rough around the edges, like he drives an ordinary car. We will have to check out his car. The car is the deal breaker for me. If he drives a nice car you can't have him, he's mine."

Erica shrugged. "Go easy Miss Piggy. We are not in a school yard fighting over dolls."

"Don't call me Miss Piggy," Phoebe snorted. "I am slim and beautifully shaped."

Erica chuckled. "Was referring to your attitude."

The whole place erupted in applause and Phoebe's stinging retort was drowned out. Erica subsided in her chair.

*****

It was an entertaining program. The male chorale gave some outstanding renditions and the other acts that supported them also did well. The congregation was asked to sit and wait to be ushered out. Because they were seated in the second to last row, they were among the last persons to be ushered out of the church.

Erica glanced at her watch; it was a quarter to ten. She looked around for him, she had been challenging herself throughout the program to not sneak a look at him again and she had succeeded. She allowed Phoebe to drag her into the parking lot, all the while looking around for him.

"I wonder if he is parked outside." Phoebe was craning

her neck over the mass of people that had gathered on the outside.

"You were serious about the car thing?" Erica asked incredulously.

"Of course," Phoebe said, "I have to determine a man's material worth before I can even think of talking to him."

"But that's…that's…" Erica stammered. She grabbed Phoebe's arms. "That's wrong and unchristian."

"You can say what you want," Phoebe said with a frown, "but I did not grow up with rich parents or the privileged life, you did. I grew up rough, so I know that poverty is not easy, it smells bad and it looks awful—it's a prison I long to escape from."

Erica shook her head in exasperation.

"Oh there he is," Phoebe said excitedly and headed toward the guy who was leaning against the side of the church hall with both hands in his pocket. He was tall, Erica thought ruefully and he was indolently looking out at the crowd. His eyes lit up with recognition when he saw them.

Erica followed reluctantly. She was sure that when they had that stare down he had been looking at her with a cynical twist to his lips. This guy was no push over and the beautiful Phoebe was going to be in for a bluff. She could already see the sneer in his eyes.

"Goodnight," Phoebe said to him brightly.

He looked at Phoebe seriously and then responded, "Goodnight."

He didn't shift from his stance and looked at both of them expectantly, as if he was on the verge of being entertained.

Erica's hackles began to rise. Who does he think he is? Did he think that he was the king and she and Phoebe were the court jesters?

"Let's go, Phoebe," Erica said roughly. She was strangely

attracted to this man, even though he had that haughty attitude.

"No," Phoebe said defiantly to Erica.

"Where's your car?" Phoebe asked Caleb.

He looked at Phoebe, a smirk across his lips. "I don't drive; don't have a job or any source of income."

Phoebe gasped, "I didn't ask you any of that."

He gave a nasty laugh and sauntered off.

"He is rude and crude," Phoebe was sputtering, a look of horror across her face. "Did I ask him anything about money or a job?"

Erica was struggling hard not to laugh but the laughter erupted from her lips, and she had to lean on the wall where he had been standing. She laughed so hard that she had to wipe the tears from her cheeks.

"Pheebs," Erica was almost wheezing, "what about, what's your name? Is this your church? Where do you live? You know, questions to show that you are interested in him."

"I have never really had to approach a guy before," Phoebe pouted. "They are usually the ones asking the questions."

"Initially," Erica straightened up from the wall, "after that they all flee from you like they have encountered something evil." She giggled again. "Let's go, the parking lot is getting empty enough for me to back out of our parking space."

Erica walked off with a sullen Phoebe traipsing behind her.

They drove out of the churchyard and turned up the road slowly. There were several vehicles in front of theirs and the road was still wet from the rain earlier.

Erica turned on the car radio and hummed along to a song.

"I am going to work tomorrow at ten, so I can sleep in late," she peered through the windshield, "then be back home at four. Being a hotel nurse is perfect for me right now. The hospital job was extremely stressful and I couldn't bare seeing Jay every day."

Phoebe shuffled in her seat. "I hate being a bank teller. I have to smile at ugly people all day."

Erica rolled her eyes. "I was sure that you couldn't be more shallow. You just proved me wrong."

"Whatever!" Phoebe kissed her teeth, then she sat up straighter. "There he is, that creature who just insulted me."

Erica looked through the window and saw him walking towards the sign that said Great Pond. He had his head down.

"Why on earth would he be walking on this stretch of road now? From here to Three Rivers is only sea on that side and uninhabited hills on the other. The community is down the road."

"Serves him right," Phoebe snickered, "doesn't even have a bicycle."

Erica pulled over beside his forlorn figure. Caleb looked up and saw that it was her and stopped. He had a lost look on his face and Erica's heart melted. Something was going on with him. She could sense his desperation from where she was.

"Before I offer you a ride, I need to know your name," Erica said winding down the car window further.

He grinned; she could see his white teeth in the semi-darkness.

"My name is Caleb Wright," he paused, "before I get in your car I need to know yours."

Erica was still recovering from the honeyed tones of his voice. She almost didn't hear him. "Oh, I am Erica Thomas and this is Phoebe Bridge."

He nodded and she released the central lock.

"He could be anyone," Phoebe was murmuring. "Haven't you been keeping up with the news?"

He came in, sat in the car, and sighed. "I have no idea where

I am going, my grand Aunt Reba lives in a place called Three Rivers and I was kind of left here by the bus."

Phoebe frowned looking around at him. "Reba Brownwell was your relative?"

He nodded.

"Well, well, well," she pursed her lips. "Did you know that it was the church that had to bury her? Not one of her family members came to the funeral."

Erica drove out into the road. "So are you going to her house?"

"Yes," he said. "This is providential that you know where she lives because I was just gearing up to walk to the town and maybe sit out the night somewhere."

"I think so too," Erica said, "because Miss Reba's place is about half an hour from here up in the hills. She definitely does not live on the main; she is way off the beaten path."

"And has a fabulous view," Phoebe said, warming up to Caleb slightly. "If only Miss Reba had built a good sized house to take advantage of the view. So, where are you coming from?" Phoebe asked Caleb. "You don't have any bags and you don't know where Miss Reba lives. Are you a deportee? Kicked out of some foreign country for crimes committed? Or were you hibernating in some mental hospital somewhere?"

Erica sighed. "Pheebs…"

Phoebe ignored Erica and looked around to the back seat. "So which is it?"

Caleb clenched his jaw, the feeling of joy that he had felt when Erica had pulled up dissipated like mist in hot sun. Phoebe reminded him of one of those unfeeling lawyers that had represented the prosecution in court. They had questioned him with the same rapid-fire questions and had the same evil glint in their eyes.

He cleared his throat. "I am coming from Kingston." He chose his words carefully. "I heard quite recently that Aunt Reba had passed and named me in her will as the sole beneficiary to her property. As you can tell, my family is not close, so the information reached me belatedly. I came as soon as I could."

"Mmm," Phoebe subsided in her chair, and the car was quiet for a while. Erica was concentrating on driving and Caleb was relieved that the grilling had stopped.

"So how much land did she leave for you?" Phoebe piped up again, "are you going into farming or what?"

"I am not sure yet." Caleb became tense once more.

"How old are you anyway?" Phoebe asked him.

Erica giggled. "You don't have to answer, Caleb."

"It's okay," Caleb sighed. It wouldn't matter if he told her anyway. His age was the one thing he could easily tell anybody who asked. "I am Thirty-Five."

"Oh," Phoebe settled back down. "You arc just as old as Erica."

Erica snorted. "Thirty-five is not that old."

She turned onto the road that led to Miss Reba's house and steadily drove up the hill. The road was not as bad as she had feared but it was not good either. They bumped and skidded to a stop in front of a washed out blue house that was a mixture of board and concrete.

"It's dark," Erica turned to Caleb, "no electricity, no running water. Will you be fine here tonight?"

"Oh yes," Caleb came out of the car and stretched. "It will be my castle, the first real place to call home in years. It seems luxurious to me."

He looked at Erica seriously. "Thank you very much for the lift. I have no idea what I would do if you hadn't come along."

"Don't worry about it," Erica said smiling. "The Lord always provides. By the way, since you are this close to Three Rivers Church you can stop by sometime."

"Yes, I will. Thank you again." He turned and walked up the overgrown yard.

Erica reversed the car and drove off.

Chapter Four

In the three weeks since she had last seen Caleb, Erica would think about him almost every day—*how did he fare that night*. The house had looked like a derelict dump and that had been in the dark; it must have been quite a sight in the day. She was tempted—several times—to go up there and see how he was doing, but she didn't want to seem too keen on him. He had already caught her looking at him intently. If she seemed too concerned now he would probably think she was desperate or something.

She kept running through excuses in her head. *Hi Caleb, I was just passing by.* She would have to scratch that idea because Miss Reba had practically owned that side of the hill. It was acres and acres of land. There was no passing through to anywhere but more of her land.

A few years, ago some medical professionals had gone up to the house where the old woman lived and forcibly removed her. She had been unable to take care of herself but did not want to leave her home. Her situation meant that she had to live closer to the hospital but it took two nurses and a doctor to convince Miss Reba of that.

Erica paced around the house and thought of several excuses she could use to approach Caleb. She looked outside at the back garden and frowned. It was already overrun with weeds. Kelly had asked her, just yesterday, how the garden was doing and she had sarcastically said, "It was going to the weeds."

It didn't have to be that way, Erica's face lit up, the front was also in dire need of cutting and the shrubs needed a trimming. She needed a gardener, maybe someone who could come in at least twice per week—preferably on those days when she had the morning off.

She almost skipped to her car in delight. Maybe her parents also wanted help with their garden; her mother had been mumbling that the regular gardener was showing up for work only when he wanted to. She knew several other people who would want a reliable gardener.

She could help out Caleb with some serious work. She couldn't forget how down he had looked that night, and how he had snidely said to Phoebe that he had no job and no money.

What on earth could have happened to him in Kingston that he had come to St. Ann with only the shirt on his back? She wanted to find out and she wanted to find out from Caleb himself. She had given him three weeks. He never showed up at church so now she would have to take the initiative.

She drove up to Miss Reba's Hill. She had no idea what the name of the place was. When she neared the house her heart raced with apprehension. Maybe she was reading too much into the one night she had seen the guy. Maybe he did not want her help and she had been reading the signals wrong.

She parked in the yard and looked over at the house. She could hear knocking somewhere inside, and she heard the faint bleat of a goat in the back. Before she could second-guess herself anymore, she exited the car. Caleb came out of the house and stood on the veranda, shirtless, with a black bandana around his head and the black jeans she had seen him in the night of the musical; it was hanging low on his hips.

She gulped. He was all kinds of sexy. His lean torso was well muscled and he had a slight bow in his leg. She could see that now. In the light of day she could also see that he was seriously good-looking. His eyes were dark brown and intense. He came to stand almost before her and she could see droplets of sweat all over his arms and brow.

"Well…er…hello, Caleb." Erica was blushing. She knew her dratted ears were red.

"Hello Erica." He gave her one of those crooked half smiles, which was not quite serious, and not quite a grin. His eyes were warm though. She slowly took a step toward him.

"I was driving by and decided to stop." Oh no, she shoved her hands into her jeans and tried to remember that she had decided that that excuse was rubbish.

He folded his arms about his chest and up went that eyebrow again.

"No, that's not the excuse," Erica scratched her head. "The excuse was: I have a job."

"Congrats," Caleb smiled.

"No, I mean I have a job for you."

Caleb cocked his head to one side. "That's interesting. I was thinking out loud just yesterday and saying I definitely needed a job to get this place working the way I want to work it."

Erica exhaled. "That's a relief. I did not want to offer you a job and you look at me like a crazy person and say no thanks."

Caleb nodded. "Where are my manners? Would you like to come in?"

"Sure," Erica said walking behind his long strides. He indicated to a veranda chair and sat down. The chair was made of solid wood and was very wide. He sat across from her in a rocking chair.

"You are my first visitor."

"That's nice," Erica said. Her usual flippancy was lost in shyness. She had never been shy in her entire life, and that she was now was somewhat puzzling to her. She knew several handsome men, worked around them, had them in her family; had friends who were handsome so that wasn't it. What was it about Caleb?

Caleb settled in his chair and was rocking slowly.

"So, er... what were you doing? I heard knocking."

Caleb grinned. "I've been rearranging the place, restoring old furniture. The knocking was me putting up a shelf in what used to be Aunt Reba's room."

"So are you going to live here?"

Caleb shrugged. "I have nowhere else to go."

"Oh…" Erica contemplated asking him why and quizzing him about his past but she didn't want to alienate him, she was as curious as ever though. What was a handsome, thirty-five-year-old man, doing in the bushes alone?

She looked around her curiously. The place was pretty run down. The veranda had peeling blue paint and the floor was polished concrete that was cracked in some areas and even had what looked like small plants growing through them.

"So what are your plans for the place?" Erica looked at Caleb again. He surely wasn't talkative. He silently waited for her to speak before he even commented—in the past that would have frustrated her. She liked outgoing men that she could have flowing conversations with. The strong silent mysterious man thing would drive her crazy and would eventually drive her away from potential relationships.

Caleb scratched his face and said, "Please don't laugh but I have been thinking Aunt Reba had five acres of cocoa plants. Some of them stayed on the tree and dried up because there was nobody here to pick them. But I reaped quite a lot of cocoas in the last three days and there is a whole lot more. I was thinking that maybe I could sell them to the factory in St. Mary. I heard that they take raw cocoa for a fair price, but later on I would like to process them myself and start a little specialty business selling chocolate or even chocolate bars. Well, that's a dream anyway… "

Erica was speechless. A man who wanted to do chocolate, in any form, was her type of man. She had to physically stop herself from licking her lips. Her wayward tongue was drooling and her imagination was running wild.

"It's a bad idea isn't it?" Caleb asked. A dejected tone had crept into his voice.

Erica perked up. "Are you crazy? It is the best idea I have ever heard. Do you know anything about the process?"

"Yes, I worked on a small cocoa farm in Canada for a year. I know the whole process inside out. When I found out that Aunt Reba has five acres of mature trees, I couldn't believe it. It seems as if she was planning to do something with it. Some of the trees are just flowering. It is going to be a huge job to clear out five acres though. They are over-grown with weeds."

Erica nodded. "You will have to work out some form of business plan so that you can see where you want to go with this and how you can finance it every step of the way."

Caleb nodded. "I was thinking of that." He went silent

again, staring across the yard. "Do you want to help me with it?"

Erica nodded vigorously. "I'll help you put it together. Sure, no problem."

"So what was the job offer you had for me?"

He had this way of staring at her directly in a very intent manner and Erica had to struggle to remember her thoughts.

"Oh, I was thinking about what you said to Phoebe about having no money and no job. It never occurred to me to ask what you do."

"I was a chef," he grinned, "in another life. As a matter of fact, the hotel I used to work with sent me on an intense one-year course and I have the title of Certified Master Pastry Chef."

Erica gasped. "You can make pastry, heavenly delights that will make a girl's mouth water?"

"Yes, as a matter of fact I had just finished a course in Europe…" his voice trailed away and an angry flash appeared in his eyes.

"What was the course about?" Erica asked, wanting him to forget whatever it was that had caused that vicious expression in his eyes.

"I had finished my chocolate making studies. I guess you could call me a chocolatier."

Erica was stunned, what were the odds that the man whom they had picked up at church was a specialist in the one addiction that she had problems shaking. "What a coincidence, I am a chocoholic."

Caleb laughed. "You had a transfixed expression on your face when I said chocolate so I could guess it was something like that."

"I guess it is no use offering you that job I was thinking of then."

"No, please, what is it?" Caleb asked anxiously. "I am kind of on the verge of begging for food. Aunt Reba had planted some crops but the goats had free rein with the place and they have eaten down everything."

"Well, I was thinking that you could do my yard at least twice per week. But now that I hear that you are certified in so many cooking courses, I could talk to the manager at the hotel where I work and…"

"No, I can't work at any hotel."

"But why? You have the certificates. You said you had worked at a hotel before."

"I have worked at several hotels," Caleb stood up and leaned on the wall, "but I am not working for any established business in that capacity ever again."

"But why?"

"It's a long story," Caleb looked at her and then turned around again. "Maybe one day I'll tell you. So which days do you want me to work for you?"

Erica looked at him long and hard. "If you can't work for any established business maybe I shouldn't hire you."

Caleb shrugged. "Aunt Reba has a couple of goats, I could sell a few of them in the meantime. I'll survive."

Erica contemplated him some more and he withstood her scrutiny, not backing off from his stubborn stance. What could be so bad that a hotel would not want to hire him?

She shook her head in exasperation. She had begun to realize that it was when he seemed most nonchalant that he really needed the help, and something about him was tugging at her heartstrings.

"Okay, all right. Are Tuesdays and Thursdays okay for you?"

"Sure." He grinned at her. His tensed shoulders relaxed a little. "I will need directions to where you live."

Erica nodded. "Don't worry about tools. There are a whole host of gadgets in the tool shed." She got up reluctantly and headed to the car.

Caleb watched her retreating to her car and said barely loud enough for her to hear, "Thank you Erica."

Erica turned around smiling brightly, "My pleasure."

Chapter Five

Caleb slumped in the chair that Erica had been sitting in after she drove out of the yard. He felt a relief so intense that she had been to see him that his fingers were shaking. She was a lovely person and she was interested in his well-being. He couldn't remember anyone ever caring about him enough to drive into remote hills because they wanted to know if he was all right, and that was just from one meeting.

He had grown up rough and unloved, by a father who thought he was an unfortunate accident. His teenage mother had left him at his father's doorstep and disappeared. He had boxed about in his late teens, flitting from one job to another until he realized that he loved to cook. He had taken a job as a dishwasher at a restaurant at night and gone to school to get the relevant cooking certificates by day.

He had slept in the back room of his father's rundown house in Portmore and plotted ways in which he could escape. The opportunity had come when he went to Canada on the farm-working program. He had been fortunate enough to be placed on a cocoa farm. From harvesting the cocoa fruit to roasting the seeds and making chocolate, he had been especially fascinated with making chocolate desserts.

He diligently saved all his money and when he came back to Jamaica he went to school to become a certified chef. Eventually he got a job with a large hotel chain in Kingston and made it to pastry chef.

He had gotten himself a car, bought a small house in St. Catherine and married Julia. At the time he thought that they were kindred spirits. They basically had the same dismal history. Julia had a six-year old daughter whom he had considered his child, even though she wasn't—then everything changed.

He closed his eyes. He had asked God, when he was in prison, to take away his bitterness about the whole thing, but some days, like now, when he considered that he did not even have two dimes to rub together and that his reputation was in shreds and he had a prison record, it was hard for bitterness not to rise up in him like an unhealed wound.

He groaned under the onslaught of it. He was tired to ask God, why him. It was pointless and he felt somewhat ungrateful, at least he had been released from prison and though he was sorry that his aunt had died. At least she had the foresight to leave him her land in a will. Otherwise, he would have been let out from prison with nowhere to go and nobody to go to.

He looked at the watch he found in Aunt Reba's drawer; it seemed masculine enough so he had put it on. It was ten o'clock, time for him to head down the road. He was going to sell two of Aunt Reba's goats to a farmer who had eagerly asked him if he could buy them.

He had been expecting to only find three goats and a cow

when he got here but instead he had found almost two-dozen goats and no cow in sight. The goats were healthy; they had been living on the land unattended, quite content to eat the abundant grass that could be found on the acreage.

When he sold the two goats he would have enough money to buy himself some clothes so that he could go to church and maybe into town without being self-conscious.

His black pants and jeans were looking ragged after three weeks of him constantly wearing them, and quite frankly, he was tired of eating just mangoes and cocoa fruit. He reasoned that if he could make enough from the goat sales he could buy some seeds and plant some cash crops like tomatoes and corn.

He got up and headed inside the spacious five-room house. When he had gotten here, in the night three weeks ago, he hadn't taken stock of his surroundings, he had just headed for what looked like a bedroom and laid down in his clothes.

He had cried himself to sleep that night feeling lonely and disappointed at his life so far. He had grown up tough and rarely gave in to self-pity but that first night made him feel vulnerable and alone. He liked to think of his crying that night as cleansing tears. He had gone to bed exhausted and woke up to see that in the light of day the interior of the house was not as bad as he had thought it was from the outside.

There was a large living/dining room, a bedroom, and a bathroom with one of those old toilets that had a pull-chain at the top of a tank that was mounted to the wall to flush it.

He had been pleasantly surprised to find that he had running water and was relieved in the morning to see that there was a very large tank some ways from the house situated on an even higher elevation than the house. The water pressure was heavy and he found, out after investigating, that the tank was full. Aunt Reba had had the foresight to mesh the whole thing and cover it, so the water was clean.

The kitchen was a room that was obviously well lived in when Aunt Reba was alive. He could still smell a faint garlic aroma in there.

He had felt as if he had time traveled into the eighties when he saw that the fridge was kerosene oil operated and that his aunt still had rum-preserved fruit in the pantry. He also found pickled peppers in a jar and a large jar with noni fruit, rotting in its own juice.

He had also found a linen closet filled with sheets, towels and curtains that Aunt Reba had stored, some of them still having the tags on—he couldn't find any male clothes though, even after searching the house from top to bottom.

He had proceeded to air out the place and wash the dusty curtains hanging at the windows. He also cleaned the wooden floors with polish that he found in Aunt Reba's collection of household cleaners; by the fifth day, the interior smelled lived in and clean.

That had been important to him. Prison had a certain scent that he wanted to wipe out of his mind forever. He had vowed that when he got out he would never again take fresh air for granted. The house smelled homely, like vanilla and lavender. If he had money he would have bought some stuff to cook to really give the place a good homey smell, but alas, he had none.

Two mornings ago, while exploring the ten-acre property, he inadvertently wandered onto Mr. McGregor's land. McGregor had introduced himself as a neighbor and farmer and had mentioned that he "Thought highly of Miss Reba." His whiskered face wore a broad engaging smile.

Caleb had seen the goats on the east side of the land; they preferred that section, apparently. He had crawled through the thickets to count them. They looked like ordinary goats to him but Farmer McGregor said that they were a special cross breed of Nubian and Boer.

"The Nubian," Farmer McGregor had looked at him as if he were an idiot, "is good for milk and the Boer is good for meat."

At his still puzzled expression Farmer McGregor had snapped, "The Nubian has the long ears. I have been looking in on them since Miss Reba went to the hospital."

"Oh, Thank you," Caleb had said gratefully.

"In these hills we look out for each other, and because we are so far off the path we usually have no problems with *praedial* larceny."

"That's a relief," Caleb had said, "or I wouldn't have found any cocoa or goats."

Farmer McGregor had rubbed his chin. "Oh yes, too bad about the cow though, died last year."

Caleb had nodded. "Goat milk is just as good as cows milk."

"So when did you arrive?" Farmer McGregor had asked interestedly.

"Three weeks ago...came in the night." Caleb had tensed his body expecting a long slew of questions about where he was from and why he hadn't visited his aunt, but McGregor had just nodded and patted him on the shoulder.

"Tell you what son, sell me two of the rammies from one Nubian and one Boer."

"Oh, okay," Caleb had said hardly daring to believe his good fortune.

"I'll give you $40,000 for each." Farmer McGregor had then scratched his head and said hurriedly, "Got to go. I have to catch the market truck. Meet me here two days time. I'll have the cash. Remember the long eared one is the Nubian, okay?"

"Okay," Caleb had said happily.

He was now heading to the eastern part of the land for the two goats; he just hoped the goats would corporate with him when he tried to tie them.

Chapter Six

It was Tuesday morning, and Erica was having a hard time containing herself; she had woken up earlier than usual and had even changed her outfit a dozen times. She looked down at her maxi dress. It had a purple and red pattern on it and she glanced in the mirror a hundred times, turning and twisting and wondering if she looked too fat in it.

Usually, she would have laughed at herself and her feverish personal preparations for a guy who was just coming to mow the lawn, but she realized that where Caleb was concerned she was very smitten. She couldn't remember being this attracted to anyone before, not even Jay-Jay.

She applied some lip-gloss and stood back from the mirror to give herself the once over. She looked pretty good: her fair complexion was flawless, her eyes bright and looked rested and her teeth straight and white. What else could a man want? Maybe breakfast. She hurried to the kitchen and started preparing ackee-and-saltfish and cornmeal dumplings. She was so busy she didn't hear when Caleb knocked on the patio door.

She jumped; her heart beating a mile a minute. She inhaled and nervously went to the door.

"Hello Caleb." Her nervous smile became genuinely bright when she drank him in with her eyes. He was in a white shirt and blue jeans.

He leaned on the door, one eyebrow raised in a question. "I thought I was at the wrong house, I called and called and called."

Erica grinned. "I was cooking, got caught up."

"It smells good in here," Caleb moved back from the door. "Where is the tool shed?"

"Oh," Erica said blankly. For a minute she didn't remembered that he had come to work today and not to have breakfast with her. She had been so caught up in preparing breakfast for him and the fantasy of two of them chatting over the meal that she had completely overlooked the fact that he was supposed to be working.

"The tool shed is that way." She pointed him to the back of the house. "My brother-in-law liked to do the garden himself so he had several tools of all kinds. I am sure you'll know what is what. Use them all if you have to."

Caleb nodded. "Would you prefer if I did the front first or the back?"

Erica stared at him blankly; she had been admiring the way his biceps flexed under his t-shirt when he moved his arm. She didn't want to let on that she wasn't listening so she just said, "Yes."

Caleb was openly laughing at her now. "Yes to the front?"

Erica nodded again; her eyes were skittering from his lean body to the view of the trees behind them. She was acting like an idiotic teenager but then again she was sure that no teenager acted as stupid as this.

Caleb smiled. "You look lovely today."

Erica blushed. "Er...thanks... are you married?"

Caleb grinned. "No—are you?"

"Ah no," Erica spun around to head into the kitchen, totally embarrassed by her awe struck reaction to him. She hadn't been this skittish around him before and suddenly she was shivery and trembling like a newborn puppy.

"Would you like some breakfast when you are done?"

Caleb who was heading toward the shed, looked back at her and said. "Thank you very much."

She caught herself from saying you are welcome in a simpering manner and almost ran into the kitchen—her heart racing a mile a minute. She couldn't face him again; the poor guy probably thought she was crazy.

It took her all of fifteen minutes to stop calling herself names and castigating herself. *Why oh why am I such an idiot?* She lamented.

She heard the lawn mower start up and she ran upstairs to the front bedroom where she could look over the front lawn and watched as Caleb pushed the mower through the overgrown grass. He had tied a bandana on his head. He had removed his t-shirt and was now in a white sleeveless undershirt that had small holes dotted through the fabric. She leaned closer to the window and could almost count the number of sweat droplets that were racing down his face.

She contemplated going out there with water to offer him but the man had only started working ten minutes ago; wouldn't it look desperate of her to start offering him water already? This was the topic that raced through her mind as she drew up a chair and sat staring avidly at her gardener. She hadn't even responded when the phone started to ring, so absorbed was she in what she was calling in her mind *The Caleb Show*.

When she finally went to answer the phone, it was Kelly.

"Miss Lady," Kelly was saying in her ear, "I was just about to hang up. Were you outside?"

"Nah," Erica said distractedly. "I was watching the gardener."

"That new fine guy you've been gushing about?" Kelly asked her.

"Yup," Erica carried the phone closer to the window. "He is now wiping sweat from his brow. It's adorable."

"Adorable?" Kelly shrieked with laughter. "You are far gone."

Erica snorted.

"So what is it about this guy that you really like?"

"Well," Erica said contemplating, "he is the strong, mysterious type…you know the type I like."

"Mmmhm," Kelly agreed, "types like Jay-Jay, bigamists and such."

"Leave Jay-Jay out of this," Erica said, staring at Caleb who was now, near the driveway.

"So, is he married?" Kelly asked, just to be clear.

Erica grinned. "Unlike Jay-Jay, he is single."

"And you know this because?" Kelly's asked expectantly.

"Because he told me, I asked him," Erica chuckled, "after I flitted around like a school girl this morning…tripping over my tongue like an idiot."

"Find out more," Kelly said with warning in her voice, "before you get too deeply involved and get hurt again."

"I will," Erica was once again distracted as Caleb had stopped the mower and was flexing his muscles as if he was hurt.

"I think he sprained something," Erica whispered to Kelly.

"He is stretching in the most intriguing way."

"I think you sprained your brain," Kelly said exasperated, "and you are acting like we used to at children's camp."

Erica grunted, watching Caleb keenly.

"Anyway, I got a job with this holiday rental firm. I'll be busy in the next few weeks."

"Oh, congrats hun…how are my munchkins?"

"Thea is making loads of friends; everyday is another kiddies party for her. Matthew is constantly tagging along with some church friends of ours to the beach and Mark is the most intelligent baby on the planet."

"Good," Erica smiled. "How's Theo?"

"He's fine. We are doing well. We found a fab restaurant over on the West Side. We are going to use it as our date night spot."

"It just occurred to me, that my guy was a chef. How can I feed him breakfast from my lowly hands when he is a food connoisseur?"

"He is your guy now?" Kelly sighed. "You can cook, that's the one talent that nobody can argue with. Go and show off your talent to your guy, and stop the school girl drama."

"Okay Mam. I think I am going to sprinkle just a hint of basil on my ackee."

"Bye Erica," Kelly said to her sister who she was sure was too distracted to even hear her.

*****

Erica timed her arrival in the kitchen when she saw Caleb heading to the back of the shed. She casually leaned on the patio rails. A gentle breeze was blowing and she hung her head out casually.

"Oh Caleb, do you want to share some breakfast with me

now?"

"Oh sure. I'll just put these things back and have a quick wash. The pipe by the shed is used for that, I figure."

Erica nodded. She placed the breakfast things on the table and sat waiting for Caleb to join her. He approached her on the patio once more and gave her one of his signature half smiles—he was still in his jeans and white t-shirt.

"This is a lovely house."

"Thank you. My sister and her husband built it a couple years ago. Please have a seat."

He sat down and sniffed the air. "This is a nice spread."

Erica smiled. "I hope it meets your lofty chef-standards."

"Anything would be an improvement on what I have been having these last couple of weeks, though one morning I found plantains on a tree in the thicket and Farmer McGregor, from next door, gave me two laying hens so I have eggs every week now."

"That was nice of him," Erica smiled. They ate silently and Erica wondered to herself what could have happened to allow Caleb to be at this level. She was psyching up herself to ask him about his past when he beat her to it.

"So what do you do? I have been meaning to ask but never got round to it."

"I am a nurse," Erica said sipping her fruit juice. "I work at Hotel Flamingo. This month I am on the evening shift—twelve to nine. I used to work in the surgical ward at Three Rivers Bay Hospital but my fiancé, a doctor, turned out to be married already so I left there. I couldn't stand to see his smug face everywhere I turned, so I left and went to work at the hotel. The work is easier, times easier to handle, so I'm in cruise mode."

Caleb nodded, his eyes warm. "So have you lived here long?"

"Nah," Erica said leaning back in her chair, "I was living in an apartment in St. Ann's Bay. I bought it like ten years ago. Actually, I never saw myself living in a house until I had a family but my sister and her family moved to the Cayman Islands so I am taking care of the place for her."

Caleb nodded. "This is a very nice place."

"I helped to lay the stone work at the gate," Erica sighed. "Those were the days when I was slimmer and ice cream and chips were not my constant companions."

Caleb looked at her assessingly. "You are not that fat."

"Thank you. I would hug you for your flattery but I know different. I haven't been motivated to exercise for the past, let me see," she threw up her hands, "ten years...I love pastries."

Caleb snickered. "Me too, I love to create them. I love to mix ingredients together and see the outcome."

Erica laughed. "Yes we do have that in common but you are muscular and...anyway you make it, not eat it."

Caleb winked. "You are beautiful both inside and out, no need to worry about a little weight. But if you are that worried, you could help me clear the land up at Aunt Reba's. That will surely slim you down."

"Done," Erica said quickly.

"Wha...I was joking," Caleb said.

"What time do you get up?" Erica asked, a steely resolve in her eyes.

"At four-thirty most mornings," Caleb said as if dazed. "Seriously, Erica, I was kidding. I couldn't ask a woman..." He held up his hands and corrected himself when he saw the glint of battle in Erica's eyes. "I couldn't ask a nurse to blister her fingers."

"Well, I'll be there at five," Erica said. "We'll clear the land together, pick cocoa, fix your house. I'll lose the weight and you'll have the help."

"But Erica, it's hard work not a little half hour stint at the gym." Caleb was spluttering.

"That's true, which makes it even more attractive. Think about it, if I don't do something about my weight, one day the fire fighters are going to have to cut me out of this house. You have a responsibility to help me—a fellow human being in need of exercise."

"Oh well," Caleb said contemplatively. "I guess I could use your help."

He got up hurriedly. "I'm not used to this."

"Used to what?" Erica smirked triumphantly.

"Having a female being so...er... helpful."

Erica fanned him off. "Don't worry about it. I like you."

Caleb looked at her transfixed for a moment. He hadn't really thought about it, past the fact that she was extremely kind to him, but this quirky so-called fat girl was growing on him.

"I like you too." he admitted, dazed. "I actually like you too."

Chapter Seven

That Sabbath when Erica went to church *I like you too* kept ringing in her head. Did that mean he really liked her, or did he just like her, the way you would a flea bitten puppy that followed you everywhere with a desperate plea in its eyes?

She felt like that around Caleb since the moment she had given him that lift. He was all standoffish and macho and she was all bubbly and needy. Maybe she should start getting serious. The thought crossed her mind and then died quickly, she was surely past the age when she needed to second guess herself over a man and feel all jittery and needy.

She spotted her parents in the church foyer and made a beeline for them.

"I heard you found a man." Fred was looking at her with a twinkle in his eye.

Erica hugged her Dad. "I just told Mom that I am going exercising with a guy in the morning. How does that translate into me finding a man?"

Lola laughed. "For you to get up early to exercise can only mean that you found a guy."

"Good for you my precious." Fred beamed, pinching her cheeks.

Erica rolled her eyes and swatted her mother's hand. "You are too much, I can't tell you one thing and you don't put special meaning to it."

Lola shrugged. Her hair was piled high in a conical bun and she had over plucked her eyebrows, which gave her an inquisitive look.

"Your eyebrows are atrocious." Erica whispered to her mother.

Lola covered her forehead with her fingers and whispered. "I know, my hands were unsteady when I was shaving it off. Who is that man?" Her tone changed to urgency. She dropped her hand and put on her best hostess smile.

Erica spun around and saw a few persons milling at the door, and Caleb.

"Caleb!"

Her eyes widened momentarily and then she drunk him in. He looked tall dark and dangerous, and was standing at the beginning of the foyer, dressed all in black. Already the greeters at the door were flocking him. He looked around, saw her, and then gave her that half tilt smile.

"That's him," she whispered to Lola and swallowed.

Fred had turned to talk to someone so Lola was free to rib Erica. "He's very good-looking." Lola shook her head. "He is not your type."

"Why not?" Erica waved to Caleb.

"He's too sure of himself, too something… I can't put my finger on it."

"That's crazy." Erica hissed. "How can you say somebody is too sure of them self before talking to them?"

Caleb headed over to them and Lola put on her brightest smile. "Hello I'm Lola," she said before Caleb could even speak, "I am Erica's mom."

Caleb nodded. "I am Caleb, Erica's...er friend." His voice was as smooth as honey.

Lola nodded speculatively. "And you have a lovely voice, can you sing?"

"Stop it, Ma." Erica turned to Caleb. "She's the choir mistress."

"Oh," Caleb grinned. "I used to sing with the guys from Cell Block D..." his voice petered out. What was he saying— he had made up his mind not to mention his past, and here he was blabbing about his days singing in prison. What would these lovely ladies do if they found out that he had been in prison for five years? The question had been gnawing at him for days. He had loved the opportunity to come to St. Ann to start afresh and to let his past stay dead and buried but Erica was so persistent. She had burrowed herself under his skin, helping him even when he didn't ask and now here he was at her church, instead of keeping a polite distance between them he was drawing closer to her.

It's just that she was so bubbly, and chirpy, and kind and so easy to be with. He had always had turbulent relationships with women. His mother hadn't made it easy on him when she had left him as a baby with his father. The succession of girlfriends that had passed through his father's life had not made it any easier either. His wife... he shuddered, that was a no-go topic in his mind.

Then here was Erica and her mother. The two of them looking at him like he was a long lost friend; their eager eyes flitting along his facial lines with a familiarity that he wished was deserved.

"Cell Block D?" Lola asked. "Never heard of them."

"Oh we weren't popular," Caleb said weakly.

He had revealed too much and his head was telling him to retreat, but Erica grabbed his hand. "Let's go sit inside. Pastor Brick is a relatively new pastor and this is actually the first that I am going to hear him preach."

"Okay," Lola said. "You are both invited to lunch."

"Nice." Erica grinned.

"Ah… thank you," Caleb said, trying hard to keep his polite smile in place.

Caleb went into the church reluctantly; all of a sudden he was scrambling to find the barriers that he had erected in his mind against people. Erica had found a vulnerable spot and she was trying to tear down every single one of them, even without knowing it. He couldn't allow that to happen, he had to remind himself of that.

*****

"Pastor Brick seems like he is a very good speaker," Lola said to the others at the table. She had invited Erica and Caleb—Tanya and Phoebe had invited themselves.

The truth was, Lola had wanted to get to know Caleb a bit more, but since his arrival for lunch he had seemed withdrawn, only responding when he was directly asked a question, and even then he was evasive.

Lola wondered if Caleb knew how clever she was at needling information from even the most reluctant person, or that she wouldn't allow her daughter to get caught up in another heart breaking relationship.

She and Fred had been bowled over by Jay-Jay because he was a wealthy doctor with a charming smile, but she wasn't going to be fooled again.

They had welcomed him to the family with open arms

until they found out that he had been just leading-on Erica. This time she wouldn't just sit back and let Erica make more mistakes. She had to scrape Erica off the floor and glue her back together when she had found out about Jay-Jay.

This Caleb person had better be legit, or else! She made that resolve and watched with an eagle eye as Caleb silently ate his lettuce salad.

He had refused to eat beef; said he only ate chicken. At least she knew that one thing about him.

"I like the pastor," Phoebe said, her hair was in ringlets and piled high on her head. "But I just couldn't see myself as a first lady."

"Neither can we," Tanya and Erica giggled.

Fred held a napkin to his lips trying to suppress a laugh.

"Hardy har," Phoebe snorted. "I wouldn't really like Pastor Brick because he has that little bratty daughter and he still seems as if he is grieving his wife. Besides, aren't pastors supposed to be poor or something?"

"Oh yes," Fred said, his eyes alight. "That is a cardinal sin in your book, isn't it?"

"Definitely," Phoebe said smiling. She didn't care who knew what her intentions were.

Erica sighed. "Pheebs-Pheebs, if you want riches above all else why don't you go out with Ezekiel Hoppings. He is the only man in church that seems to like you."

This time even Lola was laughing; Caleb who had no idea who Ezekiel Hoppings was, was looking at them like they were crazy.

"Let me explain," Tanya said, glancing at him. She wiped her eyes and giggled a bit, "Ezekiel Hoppings is not very attractive."

"To put it mildly," Phoebe said in disgust.

"He has crossed eyes, a cut from his jaw to throat," Erica

added.

"He walks with a limp," Lola put in.

"He has very rough pitted skin," Tanya shuddered.

"He always smells like old clothes," Phoebe looked around. "That suggestion of me marrying him is ludicrous."

Fred coughed. "But he can easily buy this town and maybe all of Jamaica too. He comes to church when he is not flitting in from some deal or the other in some far away country. The man has serious money. I hear that sheiks from Arabia come to visit him at his hidden retreat up in the hills at Hoppings Estate."

"Whoo," Erica whistled, "and he is only forty. He must be looking for a wife by now."

Tanya sobered up. "It's bad of us to laugh at him."

"Yes it is," Lola chipped in, "but we only did it because he is rich enough to take the criticism, and he is always attending church like he is on some top secret mission: sits at the back and in a corner and barely raises his voice to tell anyone hello."

"He smiled at me once," Tanya said shuddering again. "His teeth were giant and yellow."

They all laughed again, except Phoebe and Caleb. Phoebe was pushing the food around in her plate contemplatively and Caleb felt like he was left out of the loop.

"Ah pish posh," Lola said. "Let us stop gossiping. For all we know Ezekiel may be the kindest, gentlest soul in the world. The truth is we don't know anything about him. People make judgments about others just from seeing them, and then we gossip about them and then we spread rumors, which makes us a sorry bunch of Christians."

Everyone nodded and they ate in silence.

"Maybe I should get to know him better," Phoebe said suddenly.

The table was silent. Then Erica snickered and then chuckles were shared all round.

"It would be like Beauty and The Beast," Tanya clutched her sides inelegantly and then excused herself from the table.

They could all hear loud guffaws coming from the guest bathroom. Even Caleb was laughing because the laughter was contagious and from what he had seen so far, Phoebe was the shallowest person he had ever met.

Phoebe hardly processed the bedlam around her that followed her statement. She was silently wondering, how bad it could be to encourage Ezekiel Hoppings.

"Don't mind them," Lola said to Phoebe. "So Caleb," she turned her ultra bright smile on him. "We really don't know anything about you either. Please help us."

Chapter Eight

Caleb almost froze in guilt at the question. If he hadn't been the recipient of the brilliant tactical move he just witnessed from Lola, he would have congratulated her.

He was almost sure she encouraged the topic about Ezekiel and then turned to him, instantly her claws sheathed, a smile of interest on her face.

He felt like clapping bravo, brilliantly done, but instead he cleared his throat. "Well I was born in Kingston."

Tanya had come back to the table and they were all staring at him, even Erica who he wasn't sure had put her mother up to this. There goes his thinking that she was different.

Tanya had taken down her bun and her curls framed her face. It resembled a bedraggled mop and for a while, he looked in her direction fascinatedly.

"Kingston, huh?" Fred was saying prompting him along. "My other daughter, Kelly, was also born in Kingston."

"I also grew up there." Caleb searched in his mind for the

sanitized version of his life that he had rehearsed in his cell when he still had hope that his reputation wouldn't have been shredded to nothing and that a judge would see sense and not send him to prison.

"My er... my mother was a teenager when she had me. I understand that she was sixteen and still in school."

"So how did you manage?" Lola asked shocked.

"She left me at my father's doorstep and he took me in; he was barely older than her. I think he was nineteen at the time."

Caleb shrugged. "I used to play with the neighborhood children in the street where I grew up. There was no discipline or love at home. My Aunt Reba was the only family member of my father's that had any interest in me. He used to visit her every two years or so, sometimes he'd take me and I would stay for a day."

"The family was divided on some issue, which I can't remember now, so it was basically my father and me. My father worked as a bus driver and was rarely at home. When I was about six or so I made sure I went to school...fixed my own lunch and dinners. When I was ten, he brought home a woman named Miss Tilly. She taught me how to cook, and iron, and wash clothes properly. She stayed for two years; it was the only time in my life that I really had a mother figure."

"Oh you poor thing." Lola wiped her eyes.

Erica's eyes looked red and Tanya was sniffling.

Only Phoebe was looking at him with an understanding in the depth of her eyes. He couldn't fathom why the self-centered Phoebe was the only one who seemed to know where he was coming from.

"So, ehem," Fred cleared his throat, "how did you come to be a chef?"

"Well, I graduated high school but I had no hopes of going to college—there was no money. My father had moved to live with one of his ladies and they allowed me to live in their back room. I got a job as a dishwasher at a popular restaurant and then did night courses at a vocational institute… I did food and beverage management. I got a job at a farm in Canada saved all my money and invested in my education. I eventually reached the highest level in foods. I went and trained as a pastry chef and a chocolatier and worked with several hotels and restaurants."

"From that rough beginning you really did well for yourself," Fred nodded. "Congrats, man."

Caleb nodded. "Thank you."

He was just about to breathe a sigh of relief when he looked up and his eyes connected with Lola's.

"So why on earth are you moonlighting as Erica's yard boy?"

The silence that greeted this question was deafening. Caleb wasn't sure how to answer that particular question. He would have to mention his marriage, his jail time, why he was in jail and then he was sure all hell would break loose.

They would drive him from the table—sympathetic looks would turn to scorn, and shards of doubt, where trust and openness were once found, would be hidden behind shuttered eyes. That was the nature of his so-called crime. There was always a question of did he, or didn't he? Could he be trusted?

He looked at Erica, who was also looking at him. Her curiosity was very obvious. He was sure it was something that she had wanted to ask him but had been afraid to broach. He was also sure that she was happy that she wasn't the one to have broached the issue.

He wasn't going to lie; he had learnt long ago that the

truth was always the best way to go. Besides, there was that little text that one of the church groups that used to conduct devotions at the prison used to use: *Lying lips are an abomination unto the Lord and they that speak truly are his delight.* So he'd tell them the truth, if they ostracized him it was just one more group of people to have done so. He sighed; he would miss Erica though. He was truly coming to like her. She was like a breath of fresh air to his otherwise barren life.

"I … I..." he cleared his throat.

"He doesn't want to talk about it," Erica piped up. A look of sympathy flashed across her eyes and once more he marveled at how attuned she was to his feelings. It seemed as if she instinctively knew how far to push him.

He squeezed her hand under the table and she squeezed his back.

"But … " Lola piped up. Fred looked at her and she relaxed in her seat. Instead, she asked, "Who wants to taste my absolutely divine cream cheese covered banana cake?"

"We all do," Erica smiled at her, trying to avoid the —I-am-not-done-with-your-friend look.

Chapter Nine

Erica struggled to open her eyes. The alarm clock she had set for four-thirty was ringing beside her head. She wondered what on earth had gotten into her last Tuesday when she had chirpily volunteered to help Caleb at five in the morning.

She knew he had been joking but she had wanted to spend more time with him. Maybe she should call it off. A little white bird was in her mind's eye, flying off to sleepy-land, and she relaxed her body; she wanted to fly with it—soar to a restful land, forget about the man.

Didn't her mother give her an earful, when she had gotten back from the dinner last night, about how sure she was that Caleb was hiding something? Erica had listened attentively while Lola huffed and puffed about Erica throwing her off the scent.

"He was going to confess something," Lola had squealed. "You let him off the hook."

"I think he needed some space. He will talk when he is

ready," Erica had replied.

Her mother hadn't wanted to let her off the phone—dissecting every single word that Caleb had spoken and now here she was six hours later, her eyes could barely open. She could feel the chill from the bedroom windows, which she had left wide open to let in the cool breeze.

She snuggled under her sheet some more. What was the sense of exercising anyway? She was a nice size 16, so what if sometimes she looked in the mirror at her naked self and wished she was a size 4? Those days were long dead. She was comfortably addicted to chocolate ice cream—frosted cakes were her friends: they soothed her in her sorrow and celebrated with her when she was happy. She burrowed her head deeper under the sheet. But maybe Caleb preferred her slimmer? The unbidden thought stabbed her in her mind and she inhaled.

What if he suggested the exercise program as a hint that he really wanted her to lose the weight? The thought kept gnawing at her mind until she sat up in bed sleepily. *It would be nice to fit into some smaller sized clothes for a change, and to look fit and healthy.* She dragged on her sweat suit, which hadn't seen the light of day for years and was now so tight it was almost x-rated. She shrugged sleepily. She had nothing else to wear.

*****

When she finally drove up to Caleb's house and looked at the dashboard clock, it was five-fifteen. There was a fog over the yard and everything was eerily still. She contemplated getting out of the car but the place was too foggy and dark. What if he had forgotten? The man didn't have a dratted phone; she couldn't call ahead and let him know she was coming.

Then she heard a tapping on the glass and there he was, machete in hand and shirt off, as if he had been working.

Erica got out of the car and instantly felt the cold air. "Morning!"

"Hey." He had a perplexed look on his face. "So you really came. I couldn't believe it when your car pulled up in the yard."

"Yup," Erica said scrunching up her face from the wind. "It is cold. How comes you are shirtless?"

Caleb grinned and Erica couldn't help but notice that he had a nice grin in the half dark.

"I started out about half an hour ago." Caleb started walking. "Let's go, I am clearing out the east side of the property I want to build a goat pen so that I can keep track of the goats. It is up in the hills... watch your step... follow me."

He proceeded to walk briskly and already Erica could feel her heart rate accelerating. Didn't he realize that this was the first time in four years that she was attempting to exercise? She huffed and puffed and followed him as he steadily walked up hill. When she looked back she could see the top of the house. Thankfully, this part of the land had leveled off and she felt relief walking on the relatively flat area, but her shoes were squeezing her toes and she felt as if an arm was squeezing her lungs.

Caleb looked back at her. "That's a bad wheeze you have there, nurse. Are you asthmatic?"

Erica gasped. "I...am...sorry...I ...volunteered...for...this."

Caleb whistled. "This is just warm up. I found an extra machete for you. We are going to cut some small trees and make a clearing over about half an acre of land. I am thinking that should be enough for the goats. The trees we cut down we will saw into lumber to make a nice fence area...Which reminds me, I need nails."

He completely ignored Erica's grunting and groaning and started whistling a Bob Marley tune.

"The sun is not shining nor is this weather sweet," Erica said painfully.

Caleb laughed then stopped. "Do you see the goats?"

Erica swiped sweat from her forehead and took off her long sleeved sweater. At least she had had the foresight to walk with a sleeveless tunic underneath the sweater or she would have been sweltering now. At least now she knows that she shouldn't be wearing a sweater, no matter how cold it may seem outside in the mornings.

"What goats?" She peered into the half-light and saw some white looking bodies shifting in the grass. "Oh, there they are. You have quite a few of them."

"Yup," Caleb said. "God has truly blessed the three that Aunt Reba initially had."

"So, we start here." Caleb pointed to a spot. "We want to clean out the undergrowth, get rid of some of the trees…thin it out a bit. It is too thick for some of the fruit trees to grow and bear. Look at that poor mangled ackee tree…those over there are guava trees."

Erica squinted into the distance, she could barely make out which trees he was pointing to, but he sounded happy and upbeat and she liked that, so she listened to him in a semi-tired daze, almost jumping when he placed the machete in her hand.

"Let's go."

"Go where?" Erica whined.

"To chop trees," Caleb said sternly, then he started his infernal whistling again.

*****

Erica could barely move when she finally made it down to her car. She looked at her dashboard clock and saw that it was nine o'clock. The day was overcast so she had no idea that it was so late. She groaned; her hands were blistered and she could barely move her feet.

"This is worse than boot camp." She glanced at Caleb tiredly. "I am tired and sore, I can see me now, hauling myself to work in the twelfth hour."

Caleb smiled. "I never thought you would do it, or even keep up. I am sorry I misjudged you."

Erica shrugged. "No problem, tomorrow I carry a pair of gloves, water and an energy bar."

"Er, I could offer you some breakfast ... "

"No, can do," Erica pulled her feet into the car tiredly, "I am just going to go home have a shower, eat a protein bar and head to work."

"Okay," Caleb looked at her, his deep brown eyes filled with mirth. "I will completely understand if you cannot make it tomorrow morning."

Erica reading the challenge for what it was looked at him tiredly. "I'll be here."

Caleb saluted her. "Have a nice day."

Erica groaned. "You too."

Chapter Ten

If anybody had told Erica that she would have been bonding with a man while helping him clear his land, she would have laughed them to scorn. In the five months since she started to drive up to Caleb's in the morning she had lost a whopping twenty-five pounds.

Her original gym clothes didn't fit anymore and she had gone shopping for new clothes with her mother, who was amazed that she was seeing her at a small size again.

Erica was now a well-toned slim chick. She got compliments at church, compliments at work, but noticeably, no compliments from Caleb.

She and Caleb were now firm friends. In fact, she knew that she was his best friend. They chopped trees together; milked goats together. They even painted the house together and planted palm trees all along the entrance to the land after they had cleared out the undergrowth.

The place was now looking like it was cared for. The next

three projects they had lined up were to: pave the quarter-mile of roadway that had terrible pot holes she was always complaining about; rewire the boundaries of the land; and finish picking the good cocoa that were left on the trees.

She had really gotten to know Caleb over the months, though she realized that some parts of his life were a closed book. He never ventured near certain topics and she could not lead him into telling her why he arrived in St. Ann seemingly destitute with just the shirt on his back.

The stubborn silence on his part was surprisingly not a turn off for her. She wanted to know but she wasn't burning to know, unlike her mother who thought it very fishy.

Another thing that she didn't know was how Caleb felt toward her. He treated her like a good pal. One day he had hugged her sideways and she had gone home with a smile a mile wide, but that was the sum total of the affection he showed toward her. She sometimes felt like she was a chummy male friend or that she had no sex appeal at all.

Phoebe had suggested to her, with a pleased smile on her face, that maybe he was gay. Erica had mulled it over. He did say that he didn't have a rosy view of females until he met her, so maybe he really had no desire for women.

The thought had saddened her for days, so much that two days ago, when she had gone to help him plant palm trees along the driveway, she had been unusually silent and pensive. For months she had patiently waited for him to show some indication that he was interested in her but she got nothing, nada, zilch. She felt like screaming *'what's wrong with me!'* in his ears.

The thought had flashed across her mind that she had wasted her time hauling herself up to his place morning after morning, but then she looked at her much slimmer self in the mirror and thought that at least she had accomplished something by losing the weight.

She was wearing Kelly's size 6 clothes that she found in her closet and was even eating better. Her absurd love for chocolate was even waning. Maybe that was the reason God sent Caleb into her life, hadn't she prayed that she would get over her addictions? There was merit in the Word when it said 'be temperate in all things.' Unfortunately, she was having a Caleb addiction, which meant that she had replaced one addiction with another. She was addicted to his voice, to his eyes, to the way he licked his lips, to the way he walked and to that super confident smile he had when he looked at her. The man was gorgeous, she was an addict, and he didn't like her.

The prospect of finding somebody was looking grimmer and grimmer everyday, but who was she kidding, she didn't want to find somebody else. She wanted Caleb, so why couldn't he feel the same about her? She wasn't so bad, was she?

She sighed as she slowed the car down considerably as she advanced up the hill towards the house. They had painted it a nice burnt orange color, which went really well with the cut stonework at the bottom of the house. She had rarely gone inside but when she slowed down in front of the house today, Caleb was standing at the verandah doorway with a smile on his face. He was in his customary blue jeans and white t-shirt and he looked leanly muscular and imposing.

Despite herself, she smiled back. That smile really had the power to do her in. She had hoped by now that she would have developed some sort of immunity to it. After she climbed out of the car she advanced toward him. "I thought we were going to do some evening work."

"Not today," Caleb said. "Today I have something really special for you."

"For me," Erica put her hand on her heart. "Oh something smells ridiculously good."

"Well, I started out working for you," Caleb said seriously.

"Which you still do." Erica pointed out, "without pay though, which I don't understand."

"That's because you ended up working for me and you do far more than mowing the lawn at your house. I couldn't in all good conscience take your money."

Erica shrugged. "That's fine. Let's talk about what you have for me."

"Well," Caleb said, "come on in."

Erica walked behind him slowly. She had little occasion to go into the house before now. They would usually sit and talk outside after they were done working and then she would head home. The place looked a lot larger than the last time she had looked inside, probably because Caleb had painted it a soft cream color, which went very well with the super shine hardwood floor.

"In here looks gorgeous," Erica said excitedly. "You have really spruced up the place."

"Thank you kind ma'am." Caleb indicated to the table. "Your four-course dinner awaits."

Erica squealed. "You cooked for me?"

"Yes I did," Caleb headed to the kitchen. "Please have a seat. I would have lit a candle but I forgot to get one at the supermarket."

Erica headed to the table with her mouth opened; she snapped it closed and murmured. "Gorgeous utensils, scrumptious smelling food."

"Aunt Reba's silverware," Caleb said from the kitchen, "and most of the food came from the land. He came out of the kitchen with a smile in his eyes. I was just checking on dessert. I think it would make a wonderful addition to the meal. I figured you wouldn't mind since you are so slim and all."

"You noticed!" Erica squealed.

Caleb nodded. "There is little about you I don't notice, Erica."

He said it so gently that for a moment Erica stared at him transfixed. Did this mean that he liked her as a potential partner?

She cut eye contact with him and turned back to her empty plate. "So what is that?" She pointed to a dish with what looked like dainty golden fried fish with a side sauce.

"Let's pray before we begin..." Caleb said solemnly.

Erica nodded.

"Okay, your hors d'oeuvres is fish fingers with dill tartar sauce. Enjoy."

Erica grinned. "Okay master Chef. She took up the fish and dipped it into the sauce," her eyes widened and then closed in pleasure.

Caleb nodded, satisfied that she was enjoying the food. She groaned in pleasure all the way through the platter.

"You really can cook," Erica said wiping her mouth with a napkin.

"I know and thank you," Caleb looked at her intently. "When I first arrived in St. Ann it was a bit hectic. I had an overgrown yard, no money, and no friends, and then I met a girl named Erica... would you like to try the jerked chicken, mashed potato, and corn salad?"

Erica groaned in her head. *Then you met Erica and what?*

"Erica?" Caleb asked. "Don't tell me you are full already?"

"No...No," Erica started sharing the food onto her plate, "I was just wondering, after you met Erica, what?"

"Oh," he sighed, "I think you are a great friend."

Erica slowly put down her fork. "Is that all I am to you?"

Caleb looked at her seriously and then looked away. "I have never really talked about why I came to St Ann, destitute and with only the clothes on my back. You have never pressed and I am grateful for that."

Erica nodded. "I thought you would say something when you are good and ready."

Caleb sighed. "I have dreaded having this conversation with you."

"Just tell me," Erica said exasperated. "How bad can it be?"

Caleb shrugged. "Bad enough." Then he gave her one of his lopsided smiles. "Eat up, this is actually my way of saying how special you are. I never just cook for any woman you know."

Erica smiled. "Uhm, I was wondering…are you gay?"

Caleb's eyes widened in shock. "No, why would you think that?"

"Because you have never really… do you like me like a girl you are attracted to or just like a buddy who helps you clean?"

Caleb laughed. "I like you too much Erica. I am actually happy that I have so many tasks to do around the house so that I don't have to sit and mope about our differences."

Erica's heart leapt with joy, her brown eyes lit up and she exhaled loudly. "That's a relief. For a moment there I thought I was pursuing you like a hungry puppy and you didn't feel anything for me at all. What differences are you talking about?"

"Well let's see," Caleb scratched his chin. "You are a lovely respectable woman with a generous heart. You are beautiful both inside and out. People like you; a room comes alive when you walk in it. The crowd sways toward you."

Erica started to fan with her napkin. "Go on…"

"You are from a stable family background with a rich father who has a chain of supermarkets and a mother who makes perfume in her spare time. They love you and are protective of you. You are saving up to buy a house and you have a career."

Caleb got up from the table. "I am broke, I have no job, only a business plan floating around in my head and most importantly I don't have good relationships with women."

He started pacing. "My mother, my father's girlfriends, my own relationships in the past," then he said quietly, "my ex-wife."

Erica was speechless. "You have a wife?"

Caleb chuckled bitterly. "She's an ex."

Then he came and sat at the table. "This is edging closer to that conversation I don't want us to have."

Erica swallowed nervously. "This explains a lot."

"Not really. Until you came into my life, I hated all women bitterly. I remembered praying to God one night, asking him to show me a way to get the bitter evil thoughts about women out of my head. I lumped all women into one category. They can't be trusted, and they were a waste of space, but then came Erica. She accepted me wholeheartedly, without conditions, and at first I looked and looked for some flaw but I really couldn't find any."

Erica's eyes pleaded with him. "So why are you keeping me at arms length. In case you haven't noticed, I'm not getting any younger." She grinned at that and then looked a worried Caleb in the eyes. "The point is, you have ambition…at least you share some of your dreams with me. You want to have a better future; I understand that…I can work with that. My family background shouldn't be an issue. Usually my parents are content to let me choose who I want to be with. I would live in a tent with you in the back of a dumpster if you wanted me to."

Caleb held her hand and squeezed it. He opened his mouth and then squeezed her hand again with a sigh. "Let us finish our meal. I have a surprise for you."

Erica closed her eyes in frustration. "Okay."

They ate in silence and then Caleb excused himself and went into the kitchen. He returned with two dessert plates, a piece of chocolate ganache on each.

"Wooh la la," Erica whistled. "You made chocolate ganache."

Caleb placed it before her. "I was planning to wait for your birthday next month but I couldn't wait. The chocolate came from the cocoa that you helped to pick and the cream came from the goats."

Erica licked her lips and dug into the gooey rich dessert. "You really are an outstanding pastry chef," she said after licking clean the spoon she had dug into the chocolate.

"I really am," Caleb said longingly. "When I made this I missed the kitchen desperately."

"Why won't you work for a hotel?" Erica asked him seriously. When she asked him in the past he usually clammed up. She tensed in anticipation of his answer.

"My reputation is in shambles," Caleb said solemnly.

Erica waited for him to elaborate but didn't push, she wanted to know what could be so bad that he didn't want to work in a hotel ever again—she felt like shaking the information out of him.

However, she realized that Caleb wasn't very talkative about his past or his emotions and she feared that if she pushed too hard he would push her away. For months she had been waiting for some indication that he found her attractive but now that she had it she realized that pushing him wouldn't be a good thing—she felt like screaming. The tension in the room kicked up a notch as she waited for him to elaborate.

She threw up her hand in the air. "You are taking this avoidance thing too far."

She saw his expression tighten and she grunted. "Is there anymore ganache in the kitchen?"

"Sure," Caleb said sighing in relief. "You have worked very hard on your new figure, don't spoil it."

"I won't," Erica said heading for the kitchen, "besides we still have a lot of work to do on your land, I can always burn off the calories."

Chapter Eleven

It was a Thursday, Erica's day off from work; she spent it tidying up the house. It was amazing to her how much dust accumulates in a place when it's neglected. She was in the process of cleaning the master bedroom when she heard a car drive up in the driveway. When she peered through the window, she saw that it was her father. He was clad in his regular golfing outfit of polo shirt, khaki pants, and a hat that read 'hole in one'. He looked over the yard and then looked up at the window.

"Come and open the front door, Erica, and stop peeping at me through the window."

"How did he even know I was peeping," Erica mumbled. She could never get anything to slip by her father when she was growing up and it seemed he still had that uncanny knack of knowing her every move.

She hurried to the front door. She was in one of Kelly's old singlet tops and shorts. "Morning," Fred grunted. "I see the young man that you hired is doing a good job with the yard."

"Morning to you too my darling. I have not seen you for two weeks. How are you doing?" She mocked her father and headed to the kitchen.

Fred scratched his head. "I spoke to you yesterday. You were heading home from that man's house again. So what if he made you chocolate ganache, we still don't know anything much about him."

"Ah Dad," Erica frowned, "did Mom put you up to this?"

"More or less," Fred said sitting down at the bar and removing his cap. "I was on my way to golf with Herbie and King when she started harping on and on about you and this man you are seeing. She ordered me to talk some sense into you."

Erica giggled. "You may proceed."

"Well er..." Fred sighed, "I have never been good at these little female issues that are so important to your mother, but since I am being blamed for the sins of my youngest...her cheating on her husband and having her lover's baby..."

"She blamed you for that?" Erica asked. "Is Mom sniffing something?"

"No, actually it was my golf playing that was to be blamed. If I wasn't so obsessed with golf my daughters would be fine and life would be perfect. There would be no crime and all men would live in peace."

Erica laughed. "Would you like something to eat?"

"Nah," Fred said fanning her off, "this is a brief visit. I just wanted to ask... is this man genuinely converted? I mean, he comes to church but do you know if he loves God? Or is he looking for handouts from the church, and more particularly... you."

"I think he is genuine," Erica said earnestly. "We pray together in the mornings before we start working and he talks about God as if he has a true connection with him. He doesn't swear…he is always polite and I am dying for him to make an indecent advance on me."

Fred's eyes widened. "Okay, but why is he using you in the bushes as his day worker? What's so secretive about his past that we can't know? Suppose he is a cunning user, like that guy Jay-Jay that you were so into two years ago?"

Erica shook her head. "Jay-Jay was willing to get married even though he was already married because I told him no sex before marriage. Jay-Jay was on a different plane of existence. I think Caleb has been hurt before and is just extremely cautious with people, especially women."

"You sure know how to pick them," Fred said standing up. He walked toward Erica and stopped before her. "I love you," he gripped her shoulders, "no matter how old you get you are still daddy's little girl."

"I know. I love you too."

"That's why," Fred said, "I am going to order a background check into this guy, Caleb Wright." He headed for the door. "Have a nice day hun." He put the cap back on his head.

"But Daddy…" Erica protested. "I don't want that. I want him to tell me what is going on."

Fred chuckled. "That's the difference between me and you, darling. I love you, not Caleb. Your welfare is more important to me than anything. When I hear something from the private investigator I will let you know." He walked out the house, a skip to his step.

"Well thanks a bunch, Mom." Erica mumbled to herself. Her mother knew exactly what she was doing when she sent her father on this guilt trip.

But when she sat down for a while and thought about it, it wouldn't be so bad to know what Caleb's secret was about, it would make her life a lot easier if she knew what she was dealing with.

*****

Caleb was sitting under a cocoa tree, its shade offering him some reprieve from the relentless sun. He was contemplating his options. Last night when he had cooked that dinner for Erica it brought him back to a peaceful place, a place that he was comfortable in, a place he loved. He loved being a chef, he loved working with food, throwing ingredients together, and creating a masterpiece. Cooking was an art and he loved that medium of expressing himself.

He looked up into the cocoa tree. As much as he was enjoying the farming that he has been doing in the last couple of months, he was much more comfortable in the kitchen. Initially, when he had seen the acres of cocoa he was excited about harvesting and processing it and everything that came along with the process, but now he realized that what he had been really excited about was the end of the process when he had pure rich chocolate and turning it into decadent treats.

It was now solidified in his mind—he wanted to cook. That's what he wanted to do forever; it was his life's calling. There was nothing that could quite get his adrenalin flowing like a busy kitchen. He sighed. He had plenty of cocoa on the trees. He needed to find out from Farmer McGregor how to get it to the factory.

When he sold them, he needed to explore some more options for work. He could always start his own restaurant or face the music by applying to one of those hotels and enduring their questions about his five year gap in employment. Not every employer was as conscientious with police records as he had feared. Maybe he could get by until someone in HR found out. Then he was sure he would be in trouble, no hotel would willingly hire an ex-con.

He remembered when he was head chef at one of the prominent hotels in Kingston, one young man, a sous chef, had somehow slipped under the radar with his criminal record. When Human Resources found out he was called to a meeting where they discussed firing him. Though he had begged for the guy, the hotel had been adamant that he had to go.

"It would not be good for our reputation if he continues here." The HR manager had looked through her glasses at him. "He was in prison for stealing. Can you imagine if we let down our guard around him, he would rob us blind."

Caleb was given the responsibility to tell the young man of their decision. He could still remember the pain on his face and his departing words while he packed his belongings. "Once a sinner always a sinner."

He sighed. He couldn't allow himself to accept that doctrine; his motto was once a sinner there is a savior. However, he needed to do something; he couldn't just drift with the tides, stay up in the bushes, and hibernate.

He had serious feelings for Erica, but he didn't know if it was love. He had never really felt this way about someone before, not even Julia. He knew he felt protective toward Erica. Her smile made him feel all soft inside; he loved her sense of humor and her intelligence. When he touched her, even accidentally, certain parts of his anatomy reminded him that he was alive, and even more so since he hadn't touched a woman in six years.

He understood that he had to do something about his present circumstance; a man had a need to be a provider. He wouldn't allow her to be the one carrying the financial burden in their relationship.

She had helped him enough, even if she didn't realize it. She had saved him loads of money by just coming up in the mornings and helping him to clear out the undergrowth. He did not know any woman who was willing to do that for a guy. That alone made her remarkable and there was a little fear inside him that said that she was too good for him.

Maybe if he had a job and earned some money he would see himself as good enough for Erica. Maybe if they never talk about that little issue of his imprisonment then he could propose to her. They could have a small wedding and then live in the hills. He could give her those babies she was craving for and they'd live happily together.

Erica would love that. She wore her emotions on her sleeve and if that failed, she'd just straight out tell him what she thought. He knew she wanted him to take their relationship further but his past was holding him back.

He could still feel the leg cuffs that they had slapped on his ankles, and that ominous looking handcuff that they had put on his wrist, and the hard accusing looks that the policemen had given him when they threw him in the jail cell.

"People like you should rot in hell. Jail is too good for you," The policeman had said to him when they carted him off to prison.

His head hurt when he thought about it and a vestige of fear held him in the position he was sitting long after he should have gotten up.

Chapter Twelve

Caleb had never gone over to Farmer McGregor's house by way of the front entrance. He had walked all the way down hill for about a mile before he found the entrance to the house.

It was a sprawling mansion and Caleb was taken aback. His perception of the short farmer with the Santa Claus beard and a twinkle in his eye was shattered. Apparently, Farmer McGregor was one of those rich farmers who probably dabbled into farming for fun.

He made that judgment and then immediately chastised himself for it. He had realized long ago, when he had been sitting in prison for what he thought was for the rest of his life, that one shouldn't judge a person by what he had or how he looked.

The trepidation with which he had started to approach the wrought iron gate dissipated somewhat with that little speech. He pressed the buzzer that was on one of the gate columns and then the gates swung open.

He walked up the driveway toward a fountain shaped like a little boy with a jar in his hand. The house was white and imposing. Two palm trees were planted at the entrance and it gave the entryway a warm feel.

The place looked like a hotel he had worked at when he was a junior chef in Ottawa, Canada, especially with the tulips of various colors proudly waving their beautiful heads in the gentle breeze.

The garage, which he could see from where he stood, had at least three antique cars—he spotted a 1974 Ferrari GTS. He had only ever spotted one downtown Vancouver and he stared transfixed at it for a while, until Farmer McGregor cleared his throat. "I bought that in 1974, after saving up for two years. I paid £5,500 for it. I wanted to impress a girl named Sara Greening. She was the most beautiful girl in St. Ann."

He laughed and his eyes twinkled. "She rejected me for another, and alas, after that I went into a drunken stupor, picked up the ugliest girl in St. Ann and married her."

"Huh?" Caleb asked him, was he calling his wife ugly.

"Stop telling tales," an attractive middle-aged woman called from the verandah. Caleb spun around and she waved.

"That's the wife," Farmer McGregor said wiping his eyes. "Turns out she wasn't so ugly after all."

"Oh," Caleb grinned, "hello Mrs. McGregor."

She came out to them and shook his hand. "Call me Dina. I have heard so much about you."

"You have?" Caleb asked, puzzled.

"Oh yes," Dina nodded. "I used to make it a point of duty to visit Reba every Wednesday. The foolish old biddy refused to leave that house until we practically dug her out of there. She was quite concerned about your future after the jail fiasco and she was determined that you could at least have something when you got out."

"You know about that?" Caleb was alarmed.

"Of course we do," Farmer McGregor looked at him knowingly, "and we have always believed your Aunt's version of events. I see she was right."

Caleb nodded. "She was. I lost touch with her before I went to prison. I can vaguely recall her being at the courthouse at my first hearing. I was so distressed at the time that I don't even remember talking to her."

"She remembered talking to you though, begged us to help." Farmer McGregor kissed his teeth. "I am afraid the decision was made before you even entered court. That's the way of those things."

Caleb shrugged. "I am just happy God allowed justice to be done."

"I must say," Farmer McGregor caressed his beard, "it was a miracle, was it not? How everything came together for you."

"I would say so," Dina said pleasantly. "Would you like to come in?"

"Well, I came to ask Farmer Mack for some advice about the acres of cocoa I have. There are lots of cocoas on the trees, still unpicked."

"Come on in," Dina said. "I can fix you some refreshments. I was very anxious to welcome you into the community but Mackie here said I shouldn't smother you…wait for you to come around. I am so happy you are visiting today."

Caleb nodded and walked behind Dina. She was a small woman with cropped gray curls. She was very slim and moved with elegance. She had turned kindly brown eyes upon him and he wondered, idly, if all the women in St. Ann were this nice.

The women at church had been very kind to him so far, and then there was Erica—the sweetest of them all. This now seemed to have been the best place to come back to in order to restore his trust in women.

He entered the massive living room; the cottage where he now lived could probably fit in it. The living room had a cathedral ceiling and he looked up at it in awe.

"It's impressive, right?" A girl said to him from one of the overstuffed sofas.

He looked at her; she was in a gray tracksuit and her toenails were painted black, she had a tattoo at the side of her cheek in the shape of a musical note. She also had long dreadlocks, which was dyed a fiery red.

He swallowed. "Well the whole place is impressive. I used to think Farmer Mack was a humble farmer."

"I am a humble farmer." Farmer Mack came to stand beside him.

"Have a seat. That's my youngest, Priscilla. She looks wild but she is really just crying out for attention...she fancies herself a female Bob Marley. Dina and I managed to have only two biologically but we have eight children in all. Excuse me for a few minutes, I promised to call my oldest, to offer him some advice. He's the one I bought the goats for. He's experimenting with a goat farm, trying to walk in his Pa's footsteps."

"Okay." Caleb sat down across from Priscilla and she looked at him assessingly.

"So where have you been hiding?"

"Hiding? Well I haven't been hiding, I've been next door."

"Oh, so how was prison?"

"Well," Caleb said hesitating, all this time he was sitting at home nervous about his reputation when apparently Farmer McGregor and his family were well aware of his past. "It was tough, try not to go there." Caleb added, "One would expect to talk about the weather with a stranger, not one's prison experience."

Priscilla brushed him off with a wave. "So are you lonely next door or have you already found somebody? I know prison can be hard on a man." She winked at him suggestively.

"I am fine," Caleb said frankly. "I became a Christian in prison, promised the Lord, that I would be celibate until I found the right woman."

She giggled then stood up. "The Lord has heard your prayers, Caleb. Here I am, at your service. Should I follow you home or do you want to follow me to my room?"

"Sit down." Dina said coming into the room with a tray.

"Sorry about her, Caleb. She might look like a hard necked prostitute but Prissy is just sixteen."

"I am of age," Priscilla grumbled, sitting down. "I can have men in my room even if they are recently out of prison."

Dina ignored her. "She's trying to get some reaction from Mackie and myself with her new found brashness. We told her to stop but she continues with even more of her gimmickry. We are waiting for the good manners and moral principles we taught her to kick in."

Caleb exhaled. "Well that's okay then."

"I am adopted," Priscilla said to Caleb. "That should please you Mother, that I'm not yours, biologically."

Dina snorted. "Adopted or biological you are my child, you belong to me and though over the past two years you have been throwing a tantrum over being adopted," she sighed, "one day you'll get over it."

Caleb cleared his throat, trying to defuse the tension that he sensed in the room. "This is a nice house."

"Oh thank you," Dina smiled. "How is your property doing? Have you cleaned up the place yet?"

"Almost finished," Caleb said, "a friend of mine is helping me."

"That's good that you have found a friend to help. It is a large place. How many acres is it again?"

"Ten." Caleb glanced at Priscilla furtively. She was caressing her breasts and doing acrobatics with her tongue.

Dina said, "You have property and a good crop of goats, that's a lot to own when you have to start life all over again. I think Reba started that cocoa farming because she wanted you to have something if you ever came out."

Caleb turned to Dina fully because he saw Priscilla from the corner of his eyes taking off her sweatshirt top. "I am very thankful to God for his blessings and I had no idea Aunt Reba had thought of me that way."

Dina nodded. "She said she has always regretted not taking you when your father was left alone to care for you as a baby. She was always so busy." She poured some lemonade from the fancy pitcher she had on the tray and handed Caleb a glass.

"Prissy dear," Dina said to Priscilla conversationally.

"Yes," Priscilla said, her top was now off, revealing a tiny pink tank top that was barely keeping in her generous breasts.

"Why are you removing your clothes in the living room?"

"I am hot," Priscilla said, bracing her chest in Caleb's direction.

"Well," Dina got up, with a pitcher of lemonade in her hand, "you won't mind if I throw this over you, you are acting as if you are in heat. You are making our guest uncomfortable."

Priscilla got up. "Do you see that, Caleb? They abuse me here daily. Do you want to rescue me from this hellhole?"

Dina snorted. "Go to your room, young lady."

"You are abusing me. It's because I am adopted, isn't it?" She grabbed her sweatshirt and huffed. "One day I am going to run away and go live with Caleb."

Caleb sat up, a look of sheer alarm in his eyes. He didn't trust young girls, probably never will ever again, and to have one with an apparent crush on him offering herself in such a blatant manner was enough to make him sweat, and worry.

Dina read his nervousness and quietly said when Priscilla huffed out of the room. "Don't worry about it, she is harmless, her only fault really is that she is unsure of where her place is in life, and she is a walking ball of raging hormones. We have five girls; we have been through this so many times in different forms."

Caleb nodded as if he understood, but all he could see in his mind's eye was one particular girl, age eleven, her beady little accusatory eyes staring at him from the comfort of a courtroom witness stand. He tightened his grip around the glass that he was holding and silently reminded himself that not all women were terrible.

Chapter Thirteen

It was with deep relief that Caleb sat across Farmer Mack in a large office lined with books. Some of them were paperbacks but most were hardback, large print editions.

He found the laid back approach that Dina was using with Priscilla unacceptable. What that girl needed was a good spanking, not the mumbo jumbo about her remembering good values and principles.

Society was going to hell in a barrel because of the new way of dealing with children. They had too much power, and as far as he was concerned, they were too aware of that power.

He clenched his fist and stopped the memories of his life with Julia and Colleen from rising to the fore again. Today was really shaping up to be a revelation. It's as if his memory valve was now opening and all that was locked away about his life with Julia was now trickling through to his consciousness.

Pretty soon the trickle would turn into a river and he didn't want to be around people when it was released. He needed to be on his knees, prostate before God, asking him once more to help him deal with the feelings of rage and bitterness that the past brought up.

"Yes, yes," Farmer McGregor was looking at him quizzically, "you want to know about what to do with the cocoa."

Caleb nodded. "At first I thought about turning the cocoa into chocolate from scratch and then making desserts but then I realized that the process was too labor intensive and it may not make sense for me right now—I need to work, earn some money."

Farmer McGregor scratched his chin. "You were a chef, weren't you?"

"Yes," Caleb said. "I specialized in pastry but I can do basically anything."

"Well, well, that's a coincidence. I was talking to a friend of mine, Harlan Donahue, last week… they just finished a high-end boutique hotel called Villa Rose and they are looking for butlers, chefs, and other workers. I'll speak to him about you."

"Well you can probably tell him about my, er issue," Caleb said quickly, "just in case that will be a problem."

McGregor nodded. "Definitely, he is a good Christian. He understands about second chances and all of that. You being to prison shouldn't be a problem. Leave it to me."

"The name Donahue does sound familiar," Caleb said slowly. "Do they go to the Three Rivers Church?"

"Yes," Farmer McGregor banged the desktop, "yes they do. It's a small world, eh? Is that the church you are attending?"

"Yes," Caleb said. "Well the first night I came here, I got a lift from Erica Thomas. She was so kind to me."

Farmer McGregor laughed. "You like her."

Caleb frowned. "How can you tell?"

"You have that look of a man smitten." Farmer McGregor sat back in his office chair. It squeaked a bit and then he said to Caleb, "Well let me see... if you want I can send my guys over to your place and they can pick the cocoa. I could sell it to the factory for you."

"Thank you," Caleb said, a heartfelt bubble of gratitude gripped his chest. "You have been so kind, I was thinking about it the other day... when I just came here you paid me way more for those goats than they were worth."

"Oh yes," Farmer McGregor steepled his fingers. "I knew you could use the money. I had no idea that you had arrived in St. Ann and was actually surprised to see you there... it's no problem to help. Through the years, Miss Reba was an outstanding neighbor, and up these parts, we look out for our neighbors."

"That brings me to one suggestion...you can go home and think about it. The five acres with the cocoa are closest to my border. I could buy it from you, say at ten million dollars. It is a really nice piece of land; I could keep the cocoas and maybe expand it over on my side of the property."

Caleb had zoned out when he heard ten million dollars. His ears started ringing and his mind started racing.

"I know that it's a lot to think about," Farmer McGregor said drumming his hand on the desk, "so I'll give you time. But whenever you are ready, tell me."

"That's awesome," Caleb murmured, "I mean, I'll think about it," he cleared his throat.

"Why don't you and your young lady come to dinner when you have made up your mind," Farmer McGregor said. "I'll tell Dina to make something scrumptious."

"I don't know what to say," Caleb said standing up.

"Give it some thought," Farmer McGregor stood up too. "It is land, a very important asset to have in these days, and it is five acres. I just lectured my oldest about the same thing. He is itching to sell his seaside property in St. Ann's Bay but I told him to hold off. This is my number," he gave Caleb his business card, "call me whenever you are ready."

Caleb took the card—a million and one ways in which he could spend the money was running through his head, but above all, the thought that God had made a way for him was persistent in his mind.

Chapter Fourteen

It was the first time that Caleb was actually going to Erica's house in the night. He had started walking it in the evening and when he had neared the town he had almost stopped at a phone dealer and gotten himself a cell phone, but he realized that he would have nowhere to charge it.

He needed to get some electricity up into the hill first. His head was still ringing with the offer that Farmer McGregor had made that afternoon. He glanced at his watch as he turned into the affluent neighborhood. It was seven o'clock. Erica should be home by now. He had tried to memorize her schedule but she had laughingly told him that it changes every other month.

This month she was working in the mornings, from ten to six. He hastened his footsteps as he felt a fat drop of rain on his head. When he turned into the driveway it was raining so hard that for a moment he thought he had taken the wrong turn. He saw lights on upstairs and he rang the doorbell.

"Who is it?" Erica spoke through the intercom.

"Me," he said happily.

She ran down the stairs. He could hear her footsteps coming down and she appeared before him in a sheer teddy, her eyes wide. "You are in the rain, come in."

He stared at her from head to toe—maybe visiting her at night was not such a good idea after all. He ran his eyes over her full breasts and her tousled hair and her slim toned legs and backed away shaking his head.

"Maybe this was a bad idea."

Erica looked at him askance and then looked down at herself. "You caught me preparing for bed. I'll get changed… you come in."

She backed away from the door and he got a perfect glimpse at her perfectly proportioned butt. He stood in the doorway a while longer.

In the past, before prison, he would have had no problems seducing Erica. His body wanted to—oh how it did, but he had made a little bargain with God. If God could get him out, he would be celibate until he got married.

No relationships with just any woman, she had to be Godly: good values, upright, basically virtuous—she had to be as far from Julia in character as possible. He had promised God.

God had done his part. Now he had to do his and Erica was not making it any easier on his anatomy. He actually stood in the rain contemplating the forty-five minute walk back to the hills.

Erica came back downstairs in a harem pants and a flowing top. In her hands she had a pair of jeans and what looked like a shirt, she rested them on the banister and walked to the door hands akimbo. "I am as decent as can be. I won't even let you see my pinky finger."

Caleb grinned. "I was just cooling off out here."

"Well come on in," Erica said, heat traveling up her neck, "I have some of Theo's clothes for you to change into. In case you didn't realize it, you are wet."

Caleb came to the door and stood before her. He smelled of Old Spice faintly. His warm brown eyes were drinking her in and for a minute, Erica felt faint.

"Erica," a rivulet of water slowly traveled from his clean-shaven head and Erica watched, it transfixed, as it settled on his red lips.

"Yes," she whispered hoarsely.

"Would you be my girlfriend?"

"Why… yes of course," Erica said formally, and then she touched her lips to his. It was as if an electric charge raced through both their bodies and they were not even touching. They were just connected at their lips.

Caleb took over the kiss, exploring her lips thoroughly and then a guttural moan wrenched itself from him and he dressed back from her.

"Where should I change?"

Erica leaned on the wall weakly, a hand over her chest. "The bathroom is through there." She pointed to the left, "no—there." She pointed to the right.

Caleb looked at her dreamy expression and chuckled. "I'll be back, girlfriend."

"Hurry back boyfriend. I'll be in the kitchen."

Erica fixed chocolate tea. She was moving as if she was under water. Her hearing hadn't normalized yet and she still felt shivers all over her nerve endings.

So, this is how it felt, she kept repeating in her head, the raw sexual attraction that she thought had been missing with all the guys she had ever been out with. She had actually reached the grand old age of thirty-five and she was just feeling it.

She wanted to hug herself, she wanted to cherish the feeling forever. The feeling was new and exciting and words failed her. She laid out the tea cups and pot and sat down at the breakfast nook. She had turned on the outside light and it illuminated the raindrops running down the windowpane. It was a night for lovers and she felt a longing in her body so intense that she almost jumped when Caleb sat across from her.

"Your thoughts were far away from here I see."

He cradled the cup she had placed on his side of the table and stared at her intently.

"No... er ...I was thinking that this weather was a...er..."

"Weather for lovers," Caleb grinned, "you can say it."

"I am repressed," Erica sighed.

Caleb laughed. "You don't kiss like you are repressed. You kiss like you want to be set free."

Erica blushed. "I had a relationship once…back in high school before I was a Christian."

"High school? Wow, Erica, I am impressed." He looked at her warmly. "I had several relationships," he shrugged. "However when I kissed you just now I felt like I was kissing a woman for the first time. It felt new and exciting and so right."

Erica covered her face. "I don't know where to look. I am so overwhelmed."

Caleb laughed. "This is refreshing; the woman of many words is tongue-tied. I must admit that I have no experience with repressed women, but I am enjoying this."

Erica looked through her fingers. "I held out against my ex-boyfriend Jay-Jay because I decided not have sex before marriage. But now my firmly held morals are saying you are an old maid, jump Caleb now!"

Caleb took her hands. "I made a promise to God when

I gave my life to him, that I would hold on to my firmly held morals too, so you are fine. We'll just have to help each other, okay?"

"Okay," Erica smiled.

"I went over to Farmer McGregor today and he offered to buy five acres of the land from me...the part with the cocoas that is closest to his land. I was excited when I heard the figure but I'm going to pray about it before making a decision and of course I had to ask for your opinion as well."

Erica grinned. "That's great."

When she heard the figure, she gasped. "Well, that would be really good for you. You could stop this notion that we aren't equal and you'd be the real big man in our relationship, but you said you would pray about it. Listen to what God says."

Caleb nodded. "Were you going to bed just now?"

"No, I was going to watch a movie...Rabbit Proof Fence, a friend at work said it was moving and inspiring and it made her cry. I was going to get my Kleenex and one of my energy bars and watch it."

"I'll join you," Caleb said. "I am also going to get a cell phone so that we can talk, isn't that what boyfriends and girlfriends do?"

"Yes," Erica laughed, "among other things."

Caleb grinned and kissed her on the cheek. "Among other things."

Chapter Fifteen

When Erica dropped him off at his house, he stood at the doorway and watched as the car backed out of the yard. The rain had let up and there was only a light drizzle that disappeared from his eyes in the car's headlights.

He went inside the house contemplatively. He had made the big step and committed himself to a woman. He had prayed about it but tonight he had just come right out and done it.

He now had a girlfriend and felt like a kid in a schoolyard when he thought about it—like he now possessed a new and shiny unexplainable thing. He removed his borrowed clothes and pulled on a pajama bottom—Erica had promised to bring back his clothes dry. The thought of her made him smile and he lay on the bed and closed his eyes.

Today was really wonderful: he went to farmer McGregor's house and met Dina and her daughter, Priscilla, a young girl who wore her insecurities on her shoulders. *She needed to be disciplined by her parents or that rebellion could get out of hand,* Caleb thought.

His mind drifted and for the first in a long time, he wondered about Colleen. She would be about seventeen now. He grimaced. Her birthday was in February, which would be in four months time. Colleen had always loved her birthdays, mostly because he used to throw the most elaborate parties for her as he had always had a soft spot for her.

When he married Julia, she was just six. He could remember looking at her and seeing himself at that age, except in his case he didn't have a mother and she didn't have a father. He had vowed to be the best father in the world to her. He had reasoned that he could be the sort of role model to Colleen that he and Julia never had.

Julia had also been brought up rough. She had family but they were not very closely knit and Julia had left home as soon as she could. She used to be a party girl; the high profile girlfriend to several reggae stars. She had the kind of beauty that they preferred and she used to proudly refer to herself as eye-candy.

She had gotten pregnant for one of her entertainer lovers and he had dropped her like a hot potato, declaring that the child wasn't his. When Caleb finally met Julia, at a party one Friday night, she had been intent on bagging another lover to take care of her and her daughter.

He had been caught up in Julia's web and went as far as to marry her. His father had taken him aside and told him not to do it, but he hadn't listened.

What did his father know? Caleb had thought at the time. His father went through women like he did his socks. Caleb wanted a different life for himself. He wanted to do things right, so he married Julia, became an instant father to her child and bought a lovely three-bedroom house in a new housing development in St. Catherine.

Life for him was very good. He loved his job, loved his wife, and had a lovely family life. Then things started to go sour. Julia got it in her head that she wanted to do law and decided to go back to school; then she had an affair with her law professor.

Caleb remembered the exact moment when Julia turned into a monster. He had gotten home from work and instead of the usual happy greeting, Julia picked a fight with him about some innocuous topic. He couldn't even remember what it was about. Then things rapidly took a turn for the worse. Even then, he hadn't figured out that it was over. That same month, he had bought her a new car.

It was a Wednesday, May 6th. It was a rainy day and he had a slight cold, but nothing to make a fuss about or miss work over. He was at work, and in the middle of baking his famous Danish puffed pastry from a recipe that he had gotten from his Danish friend, Hans. He could still see the stainless steel appliances of the hotel kitchen, the banana cream frosting, and the giant Danish that he was fashioning when the police came to arrest him.

He tightened his eyes in remembered agony—he hadn't even put chopped almonds on the top as he wanted to do. They had carted him off, and to this day, it burdened his thoughts when he thinks about that pastry; so perfect and yet so incomplete, just like his life.

He wondered if anybody had eaten it, he sometimes wondered if the junior staff had remembered to put the chopped nuts on top—he would never know. As soon as the hotel heard that he was in court, they distanced themselves from him.

He tried to sleep after that but the thoughts were banging around in his brain. If only, he hadn't gone to that party; if only he hadn't met Julia, or seen her in her tight red dress or seen her seductive lips. If only he hadn't encouraged her to go to law school. His teeth clenched and he broke out into a sweat. If only... if only.

Argh, he hissed out loud and then got onto his knees. "Lord, I ask for your peace that passes all understanding. I have been here before, Lord, so many times, and I ask once more for your help. Only you can soothe my soul."

He stayed on his knees and waited for the peace that he asked for and eventually he felt it. He got up and went under the sheets and slept like a baby that night.

Chapter Sixteen

It took Caleb two weeks before he made up his mind. He and Erica had even gone as far as to make up a list of pros and cons for selling the five acres. They had more points on the pros than they did the cons and he was satisfied that this was the way that God wanted him to do it.

When he called Farmer McGregor, he was thrilled about his decision and had invited Caleb to dinner to discuss the deal. "Along with your girlfriend of course," he had added jovially.

Caleb decided to wear all black. His long sleeved shirt was opened one button at the neck and he folded his arms, looking out at the scenery and waiting for Erica to pick him up. Since they had removed all the trees and shrubs obscuring the view, he realized that it was really a nice spot in the hills to live.

He leaned on the wall contemplatively, *with a car it would not be hard to drive to and from work*. He could even rebuild at a location that had a better view and rent out the house. Even though he had not gotten the money yet, his mind itched to spend it to restore himself to where he was six years ago.

He had been ambitious; the world was his oyster and he had several things to conquer. He resolved to temper his enthusiasm by committing his plans to God. Anything can happen in a person's life, and as he had found out the bitter way, no one was guaranteed a happy ending.

He stared out at the greenness and a feeling of gratitude to God overflowed his heart. Over the last five years, he had learned that he was not self-sufficient. He didn't like it, he even fought against it, but God had been patient with him and for that he was thankful.

Right at that moment Caleb Wright was thankful-not bitter.

He was grinning when Erica drove up. She had cut her hair in a pageboy style and it showed up her delicate features. Her eyes looked bigger than he had realized and they had almost an exotic tilt at the side, her cute button nose actually had freckles. He hadn't realized that before and he spent a good deal of time staring at her.

"Hey you, handsome guy," Erica got out of the car. "Aren't we going to dinner?" she was dressed in a wine red dress that fell in neat pleats to her knees.

Caleb grinned. "Yes. Why didn't I realize that you had freckles before?"

Erica grinned. "Make-up. I hate them so I cover them up."

"But you look gorgeous...you look younger somehow." Caleb kissed her.

Erica shook her head. "I have on minimal makeup. Are you saying all this time I looked old?"

"Oh boy," Caleb grinned. "Your hair style makes you look years younger."

"Oh," she put her hand to her hair. "You like it, huh. I told my hairdresser to give me a Halle Berry trim to match my slim body."

She threw her hands over Caleb's shoulder facing him front way. "I am happy you like it. "

"I do," Caleb bent his head and kissed her again. The kiss had a deep drugging effect on him. He just wanted to kiss her forever; she tasted like mint chocolate.

They stopped kissing and stood hugging.

"Dinner is at six," he finally said. His hands were trembling when he touched her hair. "We have to go."

Erica sighed. "I don't want to leave your arms."

"Neither do I. but the faster we get this land business settled, the faster I can make my move on one Erica Thomas."

Erica giggled. "Let's go."

*****

They drove to the McGregors' house and arrived a minute after six. Dina was at the front with a welcoming smile on her face.

"Come on in. Mackie asked me to send you guys straight to his office. You can do business and then we can have dinner. Since it's so near to Thanksgiving in the US I got a turkey, and I can't wait for you guys to taste it."

When they entered the office farmer McGregor was on the phone; he had a pencil behind his ear and was scribbling on a paper.

"Hold on a sec, Harlan," he said in the phone. "Have a seat, young people." He indicated to the chairs in front of his desk.

Erica and Caleb looked at each other, smiling softly.

Farmer McGregor cut off his phone call shortly after that and then looked at them. "So this is Erica." He rubbed his chin. "You are Fred's girl?"

Erica nodded. "You know Dad? "

Farmer McGregor laughed. "When I squeeze in a little golf, I always see Fred on the course. I wonder how he does it with his supermarkets doing so well. When does he ever work?"

Erica grinned. "That's a question many people ask."

"Good family." Farmer McGregor nodded.

"So Mr. Wright," he looked at Caleb fondly, "I spoke to my lawyer. He said we can get everything tied up in six weeks. I will have a surveyor over the place in two days and then we are on our way."

Dina pushed her head around the door. "Uhm, Mackie can I borrow Caleb? I want him to lift that sack of corn that you almost broke your back with."

"Okay," Farmer McGregor waved off Caleb. "The old back almost gave way today. If it's not too much trouble, can you move it for me?"

Caleb got up. "Sure, after you," he said to Dina.

Erica looked at Farmer McGregor warmly. "You are extremely kind to Caleb."

Farmer McGregor shrugged. "I can spot a business opportunity a mile away: his land is adjoining mine and I have been after Reba for years to sell me some of the land but she refused, said that when Caleb got out she would let him decide. Unfortunately when Caleb got out she was gone."

Erica frowned. "Got out?"

Farmer McGregor rubbed his back absentmindedly. "Yes, yes, I patiently waited for him to approach me about the cocoas and then asked him about the land. Didn't want to rush or crowd him; I figured he'd need time to adjust."

Erica was confused. *Get out from where? Where had Caleb been?*

The phone rang and farmer McGregor picked it up again. "Oh yes Harlan…excuse me a sec, Erica."

"So it's all set then?" Farmer McGregor asked in the phone. "Good, good. I'll tell him…Five or six course meal at your house…" He scribbled down the information.

Caleb entered the room and sat down, he squeezed Erica's hand. She returned the gesture, but a feeling of unease was creeping over her—*where had he got out from?*

Farmer McGregor hung up the phone, and handed Caleb a piece of paper. "Congrats, son. I told Harlan Donahue about you, he spoke to his son, Chris, who is in charge of Villa Rose. They want to test your skills in the kitchen before they take you on. Be at their house at five on Monday. Apparently, they are having a dinner party. If the food is good, you are hired."

Caleb took the paper gratefully. "Thank you."

"No problem," Farmer McGregor said.

"Now shall we go and see what Dina has prepared, she has been in the kitchen all morning."

Erica reluctantly got up, and wondered what she was missing?

She needed to question Caleb about where he had got out from.

Chapter Seventeen

Erica hadn't gotten a chance to question Caleb that night. She was sitting at home alone Monday evening; anxious to give him the cell phone she bought for him as a gift. He was supposed to get electricity today and she had no idea if he was now on the grid. The phone was supposed to be his welcome-to-the-modern-world gift.

She looked at it again. It would be so nice to talk to Caleb whenever she wanted, instead of having to drive all the way to his place to do so. She wanted to talk to him to find out if he was nervous about the dinner that he had to do for the Donahue's. She had offered to drive him to their place but he had needed to go from in the morning to prepare for the dinner and she had to be at work at that time. He had been ecstatic about the assignment and she discovered afresh how much Caleb loved being a chef.

He had spent the night talking about some dishes he had made and what he would do to impress the Donahue's that she didn't get the chance to ask him where he had gotten out from.

The question had been riding her mind all night, so much so that Erica called Kelly to brainstorm about it and to warn her that her boyfriend might start working for Chris Donahue, but Kelly wasn't home. She was on an outing with her husband.

At least she had gotten the chance to have a long conversation with her niece. The little girl filled her in on her little world and Erica was quite happy to sit and listen, even though Farmer McGregor's statement was niggling the back of her mind like an unwanted insect wriggling in her ear.

So tonight here she was, lonely and curious. The phone rang catapulting her to the present and she shook off her doldrums and answered.

"Hi Erica, it's Phoebe."

"Oh, hi Phoebe," Erica answered curiously; Phoebe only called when she wanted a lift somewhere.

"Are you free tonight, or are you planning to fornicate with that guy?"

"Phoebe!" Erica gasped. "Can you be anymore obnoxious?"

"Of course," Phoebe said deadpan, "I have been obnoxious several times before this."

"Well," Erica sputtered, "Caleb and I are not fornicating, such an old fashioned word for a young girl...he is working."

"Oh," Phoebe said interestedly, "has he started driving his own vehicle yet?"

"Nooo," Erica said getting exasperated, "why?"

"Just curious," Phoebe said, "I could steal him from you if he were."

Erica sighed. "Why did you call me?"

"I have an issue. Last night I came in from work and Ma gave me a note and a rose that was delivered from Mr.

Ezekiel Hoppings."

"The rich guy?" Erica asked curiously.

"The ugly rich guy," Phoebe said. "After we talked at lunch I kinda, sorta decided to pay him some attention, you know."

"You did?" Erica gasped. "Pheebs, don't play with the man's heart. He doesn't seem like the kind of person you can wrap around your little finger and play your little games with."

"Well... I just smiled with him at church last week. My hat blew off, he handed it to me, and I gave him a smile. He asked me how I am. I told him I am fine... that sort of thing.

I was wondering, would you like us to go check out his mansion? I have never been up there, you know. Bluffs Head is where the rich and famous live. I want to see what I would be letting myself in for if I encourage him."

"Well, I have something to do... " Erica's voice petered out. She knew it was never okay to lie, no matter what the provocation, and her conscience was already pricking her.

"What do you have to do?" Phoebe asked huffily. "You just said that the guy you've been spending every single day with is working."

"Well, I ... I just don't want to go anywhere," Erica said petulantly, "I have the right to say no."

"Okay," Phoebe said, a sound of hurt in her voice. "I guess I'll just walk all the way to the road, charter a car to take me to Mr. Hoppings' house so that I can see what everybody is talking about. If I'm kidnapped you can always tell the police where you last heard that I went. I wish I had a friend with a car who could take me to this place but apparently because I am poor..."

"Oh brother," Erica said, "why don't you go to his place in the day?"

"It's not that dark outside," Phoebe said, "I can still see it in the half dusk."

Erica exhaled. "You are… I don't know what to say. I'll pick you up in twenty minutes, and don't believe that it's because of your pathetic attempt at emotional blackmail."

"Thank you so much, Erica. Do you have binoculars?" Phoebe asked humbly.

"No," Erica said abruptly, "why on earth would I… never mind. See you soon."

*****

When Erica reached Phoebe's place, Phoebe was standing at the gate; her wavy waist length hair out, and a pleased smile on her face.

She is so gorgeous, Erica thought silently. *She is young, healthy, and beautiful. Why am I even out of my house ferrying Phoebe to spy on someone else's house?* She was still asking herself the question when Phoebe entered the car, a whiff of expensive perfume accompanying her.

"Nice perfume," Erica said.

"Thanks," Phoebe grinned. "The bank manager gave it to me for my birthday."

Erica looked at her, her eyebrows raised. "Are you and him in something?"

Phoebe gasped. "Heavens no, the man is married and has crooked teeth."

Erica giggled.

Phoebe had a low threshold for humanity's imperfections. That is why she found it odd that she was even remotely interested in Ezekiel Hoppings.

"I was bored, that's why I am even here," Erica said glancing at her. "Something's on my mind."

"What?" Phoebe looked at her, her big brown eyes curious.

"Well, yesterday we went for dinner at Farmer McGregor's."

"I know his sons," Phoebe said grinning. "They bank at my bank; they are all gorgeous."

Erica rolled her eyes. "Anyway, he said something about Caleb being let out and I can't think of what he could have meant."

Phoebe studied Erica intently. "There are only two places a person can be let out from. It's either prison or a mental institution."

Erica looked in the rearview mirror and then stopped the car. "No! What about school? Isn't there a popular expression that says let out from school? And Caleb was studying something in Europe."

"Yes," Phoebe said searching in her bag for her pack of gum. "If your head was stuck in the sand and you were too in love to consider other options, I guess school could work as an excuse."

She giggled when Erica gasped.

"I once dated a guy who was let out from Bellevue Hospital. I met him at the bank. He was so fine. He had the cutest puppy dog eyes in Jamaica. I had no idea that he had serious mental issues. Let's just say that when he didn't take his medication he was a monster.

"He didn't like how the medicine made him feel so he started weaning himself off them but I didn't even realize that he was acting strange. I just thought that when I saw him hiding in the bushes near my yard that he was so smitten with me he couldn't leave me alone.

"One day he turned up at my gate, naked. Naked as the day he was born asking Poppa if I was at home. He almost gave Poppa a heart attack. He wouldn't leave until his parents and doctor came to pick him up."

She blew a bubble with her gum and glanced at Erica. "It's

not so bad when they are on medication, but watch out, when they are not things can get ugly really fast."

"What are you saying?" Erica looked shocked, "Caleb looks so normal."

Phoebe shrugged. "I had thought that Todd was normal too. Of course, there is another explanation for Caleb. He could've been let out of prison. Remember that night when you were so eager to pick him up and I had wondered if he had been deported? He might have been—you know—booted from foreign lands for unspeakable crimes."

Erica opened her mouth. "But that's… that's impossible. Why would he go to prison?"

"Are we going up to Hoppings' mansion or what?" Phoebe asked, exasperated. "Why don't you ask him? The two of you spend so much time together; you should have known this by now."

Erica started the car and drove toward Bluff Head slowly. It was the most exclusive community in St. Ann with its gorgeous homes and spectacular views of the sea, but Erica didn't see a thing. Her brain was churning with the question, *was Caleb mad or an ex-con*, both options made her shiver with fear. He was her Mr. Right and her dreams were heavily invested in him.

Chapter Eighteen

Erica couldn't wait until Tuesday morning to come. She had dreamt all sorts of lurid dreams. The latest one was of Caleb turning up at her gate naked and acting crazy. She had woken up quite disturbed with the whole thing, and though she was contemplating Phoebe's theory, that he was mentally unstable, she doubted it. He had never acted like that around her and she hadn't seen him popping pills.

She refused to think about Caleb being in prison—what on earth could he have done to warrant being sent to prison? The idea was ludicrous, but the thoughts were too insistent for her to take lightly so she called her father. Didn't he warn her that he was going to hire a private detective to find out what Caleb was hiding?

She listened to the phone ring and then her mother came on the line.

"Morning Mom," Erica said wearily. Her mother had been haranguing her about the amount of time she had been spending with Caleb and she wasn't in the mood to hear about that now.

"Well, well, well," Lola said, "I have no children… Kelly is in Cayman busy with her new job and you are busy with your new man."

"Ah Mom," Erica sighed, "we should do lunch, maybe go down to New Beginnings and check out Froggie."

"Nope," Lola said. "Your heart is not in it, besides his wife is constantly there these days and she's pregnant. It just doesn't seem right to check out Froggie with his pregnant wife is around."

Erica grinned. "Yes it does seem bizarre. I guess we just have to kiss our fascination with Froggie goodbye."

"Well, I have a violin lesson with one Monsieur Juvern; want to come?" Lola asked.

"Not today" Erica said, "maybe next millennium."

Lola chuckled. "I miss my grandkids. I could've, probably, carried Thea to this lesson with me."

"I miss them too," Erica sniffed. "Last night Thea told me that she has a boyfriend."

Lola laughed.

"Can I talk to Dad?"

"Sure," Lola said, "he's right here, putting on his cap to go to one of his infernal golf games."

Erica heard a smooch then Fred came on the line. "Hey baby girl, what's going on?"

"Dad," Erica paused, "did you get to check out Caleb."

Fred grunted and she heard a shuffling of the phone. "No, I have not checked back with the detective. I should give him a call next week. He said he was leaving the island on business. What's wrong? Why do you ask?

"Just curious," Erica said brightly.

Fred was silent for a while. Erica imagined him thinking

about her vague answer and then he sighed. "I am going to tell you exactly what I know as soon as I find out."

Erica hung up the phone after telling him goodbye and wandered into the kitchen. She was surprised to see Caleb outside, sitting on the patio.

"Hey you, why didn't you call?" Erica asked him.

He looked at her, a twinkle in his eye. "I was just enjoying the view and I honestly thought you hadn't gotten up yet," he glanced at his watch. "It's just six-thirty."

Erica went over to him and sat on his lap then hugged him. "Didn't sleep well last night."

"Oh," Caleb looked at her, concerned. "What's wrong?"

"Well ... how did your job go?"

Caleb frowned. "Great! I got the job. I met my new boss, Chris Donahue. I told him I go to Three Rivers Church and he was quite friendly. I mentioned that you were my girlfriend and he couldn't wait to escape me. Were you two together?"

Erica grimaced. "No. Actually, my sister had an affair with him and had his baby."

Caleb was shocked. "Isn't she the one married to the pastor?"

"I have one sister," Erica said, getting up and leaned on the railing.

Caleb shuddered. "Is she and her husband still together?"

"Yes, they love each other."

Caleb frowned. "That has to be the case! I don't think I could stay with that kind of deceit though. I would be so angry," he clenched his fist. "A child-for somebody else, while married to me?" He shook his head in awe.

Erica looked at him speculatively. "Are you speaking from experience?"

"Huh?" Caleb asked, his mind had wandered briefly to Julia and her affair with that fat law professor. He wondered if they were still together but he doubted it. Julia only used men to get what she wanted, when they served their purpose she moved on.

"You seem passionate about the subject, as if you have been intimately acquainted with a situation like this."

"Not quite," Caleb sighed. "My ex-wife had an affair."

"Oh," Erica moved closer, "did it drive you crazy?"

Caleb nodded. "Yes, I was devastated."

"So you were in a mental institution?" Erica asked cautiously.

"What?" Caleb looked at her askance.

"Farmer McGregor mentioned that you were let out and I have been puzzling about it all night, I couldn't sleep."

Caleb sighed and then got up.

"Are you cured?" Erica asked frightfully. "Are you going to fly off the handle at anytime?"

Caleb chuckled and stood in front of her. "No I was not in a mental institution."

Erica looked at him contemplatively. "Then that leaves prison." Erica said backing away from him nervously. "Were you in prison?"

Caleb looked at her for a long time and marveled at how quickly the perception of people could change. Here was Erica, the love of his life, her eyes wide with fright backing away from him as if he just threatened her life.

He would have found her reaction funny at any other time but he always feared that Erica couldn't handle his past. He wondered what would happen if he told her the full story. Would she forever have that little doubt at the back of her mind that he was what the authorities said he was? Would she believe the stories about him?

She only knew him for six months, how could he expect her to believe him when even his close friends, whom he had known for years, all condemned him—one going as far as to send him a letter filled with scornful words while he was in prison, down and depressed.

His own father had abandoned him and doubted his innocence. He didn't even know if he was dead or alive. He had effectively distanced himself from Caleb. After the prison sentence was handed down, his father had given him a disappointed look and didn't even visit him in jail. He shoved his hand into his pocket.

"Caleb?" Erica asked tremulously, "were you in prison?"

Caleb sighed. "Yes, I was."

He turned away from her and stared out at the scenery.

"For what?" Her voice was hoarse.

"I can't tell you now," Caleb said turning back to her, "not when you have that scared look on your face, like you are ready to bolt."

"Just tell me," Erica said. "I can't believe you waited all this time to tell me that you are an ex-convict. How long were you in prison?"

Caleb slumped his shoulders. "Five years, four months, three days and two hours."

"That night we picked you up, you were just getting out?" Her voice was high-pitched and squeaky and Erica started backing toward the door. "I picked up an ex-con."

"Yes," Caleb watched her carefully.

"Five years..." Erica said wonderingly. "Are you a murderer? Thief? Rapist?" She shuddered.

Caleb watched her silently and then crossed his hands, a stubborn expression on his face. "I'm not telling you when you are in this mood."

"You are not telling me!" Erica shrieked. "I can't believe this! The one guy... the one guy I thought was THE ONE is an ex-con!"

She ran her fingers through her low-cropped hair. "What's wrong with me? Why do the wrong sorts of men find me attractive?"

Caleb recoiled at that. "Erica, you are overreacting."

Erica ran through the open patio door. "I am sorry I can't deal with this." She then locked it and watched him through the glass like a trapped animal, skittish, and afraid.

Caleb took a step toward the door and she stepped back.

He stared at her long and hard, his mind warring with him. Just tell her and get it over with, but another part of him whispered. *She says she loves you and at the first sign of storm on the horizon, she retreats—how like a woman.*

He made up his mind after seeing the stark fear in Erica eyes that he couldn't get through to her and then he waved in frustration; the look of pain and frustration scorching her through the glass. He walked off the verandah in a huff.

Erica stood at the door and watched him walk away; it took her several moments to calm down. She ran through the house and locked all the windows and doors. *It was a good thing that she hadn't given him a key,* the panicked voice in her head said. She wanted to do so last week, but had resisted, thank God!

After her strenuous run through the house, she sat cross-legged on the bed, her head in her hands. Her pulse was racing and she could feel it even through her fingers. She was sitting on something hard and when she took it up she saw that it was the cell phone that she bought for him. She placed it in her lap and caressed the sleek lines on the face of it.

How unlucky could one girl be? An ex-con?

She shuddered and like in a movie she could see, playing behind her mind's eye, everytime she was alone with him; all the days they were in the hills; all the times he came to the house. She could see the two of them laughing together. She could see them talking together.

Then she saw the look of sheer frustration on Caleb's face when she locked the patio doors. Was she overreacting? She lay on the bed and curled into a fetus like position. She felt as if she had lost her best friend.

Chapter Nineteen

Erica changed four different outfits before she left for church that morning. She had been in the mood to wear black, but all her black clothes were too big for her now, so she settled on a navy blue outfit that she bought two weeks earlier— she felt as if she was in mourning. All week her mind had tormented her with the last conversation she had with Caleb.

He seemed so innocent, she thought over and over. *He was handsome intelligent and he was Christian. How on earth could a handsome intelligent Christian man be an ex-convict?*

What had he done?

She didn't want to stay home by herself that Sabbath so she reluctantly hauled herself to church. Despite the news that Caleb was an ex-con, a part of her was longing to see him and she wished that she could see him at church. Maybe then she could calmly listen to his story, but finding out that the man you love was an ex-con and not knowing what he was in for was hard to take.

So maybe she had overreacted. Caleb hadn't done anything to show that he was a criminal, had he? But the innocent looking ones were the worst. She could remember watching horror tales of serial killers having wives and girlfriends who thought they were normal.

She shuddered. Caleb often spoke of his wife as an ex. Was she an 'alive ex,' or a 'dead ex'? She had pictured it in her mind all week: the wife had an affair; he was devastated and in a fit of rage killed her.

Did he kill her as a crime of passion? The thoughts were so terrible that when Erica stepped out of her car and saw Phoebe waiting for her with a concerned look on her face, she hadn't even registered that she was there.

"Stop ignoring me," Phoebe said, exasperated. "I am standing here in my gorgeous lavender dress. I know I am hard to ignore."

"Oh, sorry, Phoebe," Erica said absently. "I have things on my mind."

"You should," Phoebe said sternly. "Before you enter church, let me tell you what I heard."

"Huh?" Erica looked at her. "What you heard?"

"Well," Phoebe looked at her nails, "Tanya said she heard from Sister Hewitt, who heard from Sister Ficoms, who just got back from Kingston, that Caleb was in prison for first degree murder."

Erica slumped on her car. "What? So I was right."

"Yup," Phoebe nodded.

Tanya who had been looking out for Erica came to stand before her in the parking lot. "You poor dear, I am so sorry about your new guy."

"Are you guys serious?" Erica asked, tears in her eyes. "He murdered somebody?"

Tanya gulped. "Murder? No, I heard from Sister Ficoms just a minute ago that it was arson. He burned down some building or the other."

"Oh." Erica put her hand on her heart, the fear she felt that her inner musings were indeed true, melted slightly under her pragmatism. "Isn't arson better than murder?"

Phoebe and Tanya looked at each other.

Then Phoebe shrugged. "Maybe it was murder then arson."

"No," Tanya shook her head, "he would have gotten a longer prison sentence."

Erica could barely put one foot before the other as she entered the church foyer. Her two friends were patting her hand and encouraging her but she hardly heard them.

When she entered the foyer, her mother was in a crowd of women, her stricken expression very telling.

"Oh thank God," she looked up when she saw Erica. "Are you all right?"

"Yes," Erica said, frowning.

"I just heard the most awful news." Lola took Erica's hand. "Your boyfriend is a bank robber."

"What?" Erica's head was spinning. "He couldn't have been a murderer, arsonist, and bank robber all at once."

"It's possible," Phoebe said beside her. "He could have murdered the security guard, robbed the bank, and set it afire."

"Nah," Tanya said adamantly. "He would have gotten more than five years."

The lobby was full of chatter and Erica was surrounded by several theories when the place suddenly fell silent. Caleb had entered. He clutched his Bible to the front of his jacket and was standing at the entrance. The greeting committee, who was usually eager to greet him, was absent and when he stepped into the foyer it became quiet. He looked around.

There were groups of women looking at him with wide-eyed fear. He recognized that look from Erica when she had retreated from him earlier in the week.

His eyes searched for her in the crowd of women standing around and then he found her. There she was in the midst of the group, her eyes wet with tears and looking miserable, *she couldn't wait to spread the story to everyone.*

He sighed and then spun around and headed out. He walked through the parking lot and then down the hill. He didn't stop until he reached home.

A woman betrayed him once more.

He wouldn't even think about it this time, he clenched and unclenched his fists. He sat on his verandah and just stared. He thought that today he could explain everything to her at church in a quiet place. He hoped that she would listen and not go running off as she did on Tuesday, but she couldn't even wait for an explanation, she had stood there in the middle of those cackling hens and judged him.

There was a pain in the region of his heart. He had no idea that Erica had been like that. This was the woman that he had given his heart to, this was the woman that had even made him love again with a depth he didn't even known he had.

He kissed his teeth, threw off his jacket, and tried to blank his mind.

*****

To say that the day had been trying was an understatement. Everyone in church had been sympathetic to her, until one little girl from kindergarten had given her a hug and asked her if she was dying.

It certainly had seemed that way with all the outpouring of

support she was getting.

Pastor Brick had even given her a long lecture after church about the sinful nature of man. "All have sinned, Sister Erica," he said to her sternly. "If a man did his time in prison and is seeking the Lord you should give him a chance. Some men have learned their lessons while in lockup. They need love too."

Erica had looked at pastor Brick as if he was missing a screw. *Why the lecture?* As far as she was concerned prison meant that you had done something wrong and she wasn't going to live her life wondering if she was going to be the next victim of a murderer or arsonist.

She refused to think that Caleb could change. *Can a leper change his spots? Wasn't he, deep down, the same creature that he was when he went to prison.*

She knew it was something terrible that he did because he refused to tell her what it was. *It must have been really bad.*

She drove behind her parent's vehicle slowly as she headed from church. Her mother had insisted, in a panicked tone, that she not go back home without security. "Who knows what he is capable of, Erica?"

Her father had been surprisingly calm. If he hadn't done anything in the past months what was he going to do now?

Erica had decided to have lunch with them. She didn't want to be alone with her thoughts of Caleb. She was angry at him. So angry she didn't have much room for a broken heart. Why couldn't he have told her about his past? He had gotten the opportunity to do so many times. They worked together, talked together, laughed together and it took him months to tell her about his ex-wife and now the big news that he was in prison.

She slumped in the settee in her parent's den, throwing down her church bag and sighing.

"I can't believe you didn't tell me about this from you heard," Lola said. "You knew from Tuesday that this man was an ex-con and you kept it to yourself? Suppose he decided that once you found out he was going to kill you? I would have lost you to a murderer that you were harboring in your own home."

Fred rolled his eyes and then sat in his reclining chair. "Have a seat, Lola, and mind you burst a blood vessel."

"No," Lola glared at him. "Erica was going to this guy's house day after day and was alone with him. She even claims to love him," she shuddered. "He even came here for lunch; maybe he took stock of our possessions and will come back at a later date with his evil cronies and kill us."

Fred laughed. "I heard he was in for drug trafficking. Not murder."

Lola sat down abruptly. "Do you hear that Erica—drugs! I don't know how I can stand this. I had a drug lord sitting at my table, pretending to be a Christian."

Erica stared at her frantic mother through her fingers, "Caleb is not a drug trafficker. He doesn't drink, smoke, or take drugs."

"They never usually do—they sell the substance, not use it," Lola said, exasperated. "How can you be defending him? Have you gone crazy?"

"I think you are the crazy one," Fred said calmly. "Did it ever occur to you that Sister Hewitt could have exaggerated her claims about the man. Besides, whatever he did in the past, he is now going to church, making an effort to change. Have you not heard of redemption?"

Lola sighed. "He's an ex-con. I do not want my daughter to get involved with an ex-con. I think you should cut him off all together." She turned to Erica who is staring at the two of them silently.

Fred got up. "If God treated us that way, we would never have a chance. In the 70's we smoked marijuana, in the 80's we had wild orgies. Remember Lola? If God had said, I can't tolerate those two sinners—Fred and Lola—where would we be now?"

Erica sat up straighter and looked at her father. "You know Dad, you have a point. I have never really thought about it that way. "

"Stop it right there," Lola glared at Fred. "You cannot dispute the fact that this young man has lied to our Erica about his past, and with good reason, it's terrible. Whatever it is, it was terrible enough for him to have gone to prison. I tell you the truth, when people dabble with evil they usually get burnt. And this man thinks that he can come to church and court one of the finest women there and corrupt her."

"Mom," Erica shook her head, "Caleb is not like that. He has a genuine relationship with God."

"Stay far away from him," Lola said exasperatedly, "or you and I are through!"

"You can't be through with me," Erica gasped at her mother, "and why are you so strongly against Caleb. You don't even know him! Dad! Talk to her."

Fred shrugged. "I sleep with her, Erica, and she usually allows me to play golf without much fuss."

Erica got up. "I am out of here."

Lola looked at her with a wounded look on her face. "If you speak to that prisoner guy I'm not talking to you."

"This is not kindergarten, Mom. You can't just cut me off and threaten me with emotional blackmail."

"If you don't stay far away from this guy, you will get hurt. You'll never be able to trust him. His past habits, whatever they are, will come back to haunt you. Maybe one day he'll get up and hack you to death, and then what, Erica? All because you didn't listen to your mother."

Chapter Twenty

Caleb went to Villa Rose Monday morning with bittersweet emotions. He had not slept since he had high-tailed it from the church. Today he would be meeting the other kitchen staff and Chris Donahue would brief them on the operations of the villa. He felt a lot more sluggish than he should and more downcast than he should be especially since he had long anticipated starting this job.

He kept remembering the fear that was in Erica's eyes when she heard that he had been in prison. He kept remembering the shock in the eyes of the women in the church lobby. He had vowed never to go back to that church; never to include a woman in his life and never to trust anyone. He had well and truly had it with women and people in general. A little pain in the region of his heart indicated that he wasn't all detached from the situation.

Dislodging Erica from his head and heart would take a while, maybe longer than it had taken him to dislodge Julia.

For some strange reason, it seemed as if Erica's betrayal went a lot deeper than Julia's. He sighed. Once more a woman had betrayed him.

Could Erica not have waited for him to talk to her? She had to tell the whole church... and now he was once again on the outside looking in. Once more, he was all alone; a prisoner, even when he was on the outside.

He didn't even get to tell his side of the story; they probably made up their minds about him by now. He would be branded and despised. More than anything in his whole five-year prison experience, he learnt the lesson that once your reputation was dragged through the mud, there was no getting it back—as that young guy had said to him so long ago, "Once a sinner always a sinner."

He tried to shake himself from his doldrums—he would be leading a staff of ten. He had a responsibility once more and was doing what he had always loved. God had restored that part of his life and he was thankful.

Dwelling on the loss of Erica and the new life he had been building in his head would cause him to be bitter again, but if it's one thing he had learnt, it's that being bitter was not what God wanted for him.

He looked around at the luxuriously appointed kitchen; it was state-of-the-art. He could see that whoever designed it knew exactly what a chef would need and more.

He ran his hand over the stainless steel appliances and was looking around at the pots and pans. Everything was bright and shiny. He would soon rectify that, anticipation built up in his heart.

"I see you are looking around."

Caleb spun around and saw Chris Donahue leaning against the door. Chris ran his fingers through his hair.

"I haven't been down here since it was built. Is everything

up to scratch?"

"Oh yes," Caleb said. "It is even better laid out here than at the hotel I was before."

Chris nodded. "The designer was one of the best." He had a far away look in his eyes and Caleb waited for him to focus on him once more. "She was truly the best."

Caleb remembered vaguely Erica telling him that her sister had designed this place and had an affair with Chris. That was before she had dropped the prison question on him.

"So, uh," Chris rubbed his neck, "would you like to come to the boardroom, I told the others to come in an hour from now. You and I need to go over some things before your support staff gets here."

Caleb nodded and followed behind Chris as he took the stairs two by two.

"We could take the elevator but we can always use the exercise." Caleb nodded.

They reached the first floor reception area and Chris led him to a door, which looked the same as the wall.

Chris pointed to another door that had the same design. "That's my office; this is the boardroom."

Caleb followed him through. "Wow, very nice."

Chris nodded. The space was painted in a mint green color and had a long desk and plush chairs in the same mint green shade with deeper green stripes. There were several plants occupying different corners of the room.

"I had argued with Kelly about the color but I see that it works."

"Kelly is Erica's sister," Caleb said, sitting down.

"Oh yes," Chris sat across from him. "You are Erica's boyfriend. Dad had warned me about that. I have been involved with that family on a personal level recently and I was weighing whether or not I should hire you because of the connection."

"I am not Erica's boyfriend anymore," Caleb shrugged. "Apparently my past is an issue."

Chris leaned back in his chair. "Surely she is not holding that against you?"

"She doesn't know the full story," Caleb said helplessly. "I went to church to tell her and when I went into the lobby they were all looking at me as if I was the big bad wolf who came to steal their little innocent sheep. I'm never going back to that church again."

Chris laughed. "You know, Three Rivers folks are not so bad. I love them."

"So why don't you go there anymore?" Caleb asked curiously. "Your father and your mother go there."

Chris shrugged. "It's a long story. I visit other churches now but sometimes I go there on Wednesday nights for a spiritual pick me up. Maybe you can come with me when I go visiting. I'll pick you up. It's not good to avoid church just because of some crime you have allegedly committed. Besides, what happened to you can happen to any man. I don't know how you survived that stint in prison and can still smile."

Caleb looked at Chris; he seemed to Caleb like a nice enough person. He remembered his lecture to himself about not trusting people but decided that he would just let down his guard a teensy bit, just for now.

"Well, I got baptized in my second year in prison. I did a lot of wrangling with God to change my heart...I was bitter. Before I accepted Jesus as my personal savior from sin I had a plan, and that plan was to find Julia when I got out of prison and kill her and Colleen, and burn the house down.

"I didn't care how they died, but I was sure that I was going to kill them personally. But God, who knows me best, sent this lady to the prison…she came to see me personally. She talked to me about the Bible and left one with me. After that it seemed as if church groups were always impressed to pray with me when they visit. The rest is history. Little by little, the bitterness went away. I think now I can probably see Julia in the street and not feel to tear her to pieces with my bare hands."

Chris nodded. "So what is she doing now? Do you know?"

"No," Caleb shook his head. "I lost touch with everybody from that very day I went to prison. I wouldn't dare to go back there. People had already judged me and found me wanting, so I have completely severed ties with that section of my life. I think it's one of God's blessings that I got this job here."

"Well, I think their loss is our gain." Chris smiled. "I couldn't believe it when Farmer McGregor called and told us your qualifications…and the food you did for us last Monday…I don't think our guests will want to leave here."

"What most hospitality places don't realize is that you may have the sun, sea and weather but an outstanding chef is the ace in the hole."

Chris withdrew a sheaf of papers from a briefcase that was leaning on the chair, "I have your two year contract here. We offer the usual benefits along with your pay package. As you'll see, it is quite substantial. We are safe guarding against anybody stealing you away."

Caleb grinned and then whistled when he saw the monthly figure, "I can go car shopping in less than three months."

Chris frowned. "Don't you have a car?"

"No," Caleb shrugged. "I walk everywhere."

"Mmm," Chris rifled through his briefcase and found his cell phone. "We can give you a company car as part of the package. I want you to be here when you are supposed to be here. Let me call Marla at our head office and ask her to add this to your contract. It won't take long for her to make the adjustments."

When he hung up the phone with Marla, Chris said, "We'll pick up your car this evening. I hope you are excited about our grand opening. The crème de la crème of society will be here. We even invited Ezekiel Hoppings and he agreed to come."

"Uhm, isn't he that rich guy who goes to Three Rivers Church?" Caleb who was still reeling at the swiftness with which he got a new means of transport, asked belatedly.

Chris nodded. "Yes, he comes by when he is in Jamaica. Ezekiel is a bit anti-social but he is one of the richest men in the world and if he recommends our villas to even one or two of his friends as a destination we are talking some serious money. This also means you should be ready for all sorts of weird food requests coming your way."

"I'm used to it. I am anticipating just that."

Chapter Twenty-One

Erica hadn't anticipated just how much she would miss Caleb until she hadn't heard from him for two whole weeks. She then realized that a big part of her life in the past couple of months had been intertwined with his. She had driven up to his place twice last week but there was no sign of him. She mourned the fact that he didn't have a cellular phone though she could see that he now had electricity running up to his house.

She dragged herself around the place and was feeling even lonelier and more dejected than before she met Caleb. She didn't even have the comfort of falling back on chocolate as a crutch anymore. These days she wasn't craving her favorite food so much.

She realized how bad it must have looked to Caleb when he saw her in the lobby with so many accusing eyes and she admitted to herself that she had overreacted when she found out he was in prison.

A mature approach would have been to sit down and listen to his story. That was what she had been angling to hear for months but now she feared that it was too late. Caleb probably had written her off by now.

She looked at her watch, it was Wednesday evening, and she had nothing to do until her lecture at the church that night. There was no food in the house and she needed to restock the pantry or sit in the house and constantly think about Caleb. She opted to go to the supermarket. Thinking about Caleb made her feel stupid and lonely.

She drove up to the parking lot of one of her father's supermarket. The underground parking lot was full and she slowly drove around until she found a place to park. She got out of the car gingerly and was locking it when she heard his voice.

It was Caleb. He was talking and laughing to a young lady who was in a tight green dress. He was opening the car door for her. She was slowly unwinding herself from the car seat so that her body could touch his as she got out of the car.

He said something to her and the girl was doubled up into paroxysms of laughter. Erica clenched her fists at her sides and gritted her teeth. *How quickly he had moved on, and what about his vows of celibacy?*

To Erica, he and the green dress girl looked too intimate to be casual friends—and when did he start to drive? She glanced at the late model Honda and felt her blood boiling when he whipped out a late model phone and started to talk on it. Erica felt deflated. Where was the Caleb that she had gotten to know?

He looked like a different, more suave version of himself. She must have made a sound from her section of the garage because he spun around and looked at her. She stared back at him, flagellating herself at how stupid she had been for not listening to his explanation. Meanwhile a perverse part of her that wanted to be punished admired his muscular physique and his handsome face.

He continued staring at her and then hung up the phone. The girl beside him was looking over a list and then whispered something to Caleb, who had folded his arm and was giving Erica one of his raised eyebrows looks.

Erica felt a bile of jealousy rising in her throat. *So, he had really moved on; they were now shopping together.* That girl was probably enjoying the newly neat place that she had helped Caleb with in the hills.

The thought was enough to make her fumble with her car keys, trying to get it into the keyhole. She didn't care if she never ate again, she was going to go home and have a good cry.

There was nobody else to blame in this whole sorry situation but herself. She had practically pushed him away. She felt a tear slipping down her cheek and she dashed it away, impatiently.

She had really loved Caleb. She hadn't cared that he was broke or didn't have any electricity; she didn't even mind when the two of them had worked so hard together to fix up his place.

She had appreciated his company and loved his sense of humor. Which woman in her right mind wouldn't have been shocked when she found out that the man she was hoping to spend the rest of your life with had been in prison?

She had been shocked, but after the shock wore off, she had been willing to hear, she reminded herself morosely.

A part of her was sure that she would have eventually found him, and he would tell her the truth about his past and they would get past it. She was sure that they could have; she was not so naïve as to think that everybody was perfect, but now it was all gone.

Obviously, he had moved on and she was now redundant. She tried to swipe away the trickling tears, but they turned into a flood. She grabbed her nurse's jacket that she always hung on the back of her car seat and tried to stuff her mouth; she wasn't a quiet sobber.

She sensed that she was being watched as she noisily blew her nose in the jacket. Glancing sideways through the window, she saw Caleb. His hands were in his pockets and he was leaning on the car beside hers.

Erica slumped against the steering wheel. "Go away."

He opened the door on her side of the car and asked quietly. "Is something wrong?"

"Why do you care?" Erica asked. She glanced in the rear view mirror to see that her eyes were swollen and her nose was red.

Caleb shrugged. "I don't know why I care. It appears as if I still do even though... "

"Even though what?" Erica looked at him angrily. "Even though you have moved on and have another girlfriend."

Caleb laughed. "You know, I will never understand women. I thought you were afraid of me. I am an ex-convict, remember?"

Erica nodded. "I remember, but not seeing you for two weeks I realized that I overreacted and I was stupid. I visited your house twice and you weren't there," she said accusingly.

Caleb stared at her seriously for a few moments and then straightened from the car. For weeks, he had been agonizing over Erica. He felt that the relationship had ended prematurely. He missed her. Several times, he had wanted to call her and to tell her about his day or just to talk to her. They had never really had the sort of relationship where they could talk on phones or go out on dates because he had been too broke to suggest it and too proud to allow her to offer to.

"I have a job now," Caleb finally said. Erica had been fidgeting under his stare. "I am the head chef at Villa Rose."

"Oh," Erica hiccupped. "Congratulations. That's an exclusive property."

Caleb was silent after that; they stared at each other silently.

"So who is the girl?" Erica asked waspishly.

Caleb grinned. "I thought you would know. She is a purchasing manager for this supermarket. I gave her a lift back from Villa Rose. Apparently this supermarket, which I understand is owned by your father, is the official supplier to the Villa Rose."

"I don't know anything about my father's business," Erica shrugged. "So are you two together?"

"Hmmm…" Caleb grinned. "No. I swore off women when I went to church three weeks ago and saw a certain lady whom I considered my dear friend spreading fibs about me in the church lobby."

"I never did that," Erica gasped. "That's what you thought?"

Caleb nodded. "So how was I the hot topic of conversation and why were so many people looking scared when they saw me?"

Erica got up out of the car and stood before Caleb. "A church sister went to Kingston for a couple of months; she told another church sister that you were in prison. I think she gave conflicting reports as to why."

Caleb cleared his throat. "So why was I in prison?"

Erica shrugged. "Arson, murder, drug trafficking."

Caleb nodded. "I see."

Erica looked at him cautiously. "Are any of those true?"

"What would you do if they were?" Caleb looked at her seriously.

"I would…er… I would… hear your reason for doing it

and…" Erica threw her hands in the air. "I don't know. I have never loved an ex-con before. I love you Caleb and somehow your past is not holding as much sway as I thought it would. Do you think I am one of those women who will accept anything because they are washed up, single and desperate?"

Caleb grinned. "I should have remembered your penchant for drama before I wrote off our relationship. No, you are not washed up and desperate."

Erica smiled. "I really did overreact the other morning, didn't I?"

Caleb nodded. "Come here."

She stepped into his arms and he hugged her tightly. "I love you, Erica."

She squeezed him back tightly. She had really longed to hear those words from him even though she wasn't sure what he had done that sent him to prison. Her urgency to know was not as acute.

He kissed her in her hair and then released her slightly.

"We are in a supermarket parking garage; there is a lady looking at us."

Erica sniggered. "But I don't want to let you go."

Caleb brushed his lips against hers. "I know how you feel, but the two of us have to talk."

"I promised Pastor Brick that I would participate in the service tonight," Erica hugged him again. "Every Wednesday night the health department will be giving half-hour presentations on health. Tonight I'll be talking about exercise. Apparently since it worked for me, Pastor Brick thought I would be the best person to talk about it."

Caleb inhaled her scent and then shifted away. "I'll meet you there then."

He kissed her on the forehead and then glanced at his

watch. "See you in two hours."

"Okay," Erica blew him a kiss got into the car and instantly felt lighter.

Chapter Twenty-Two

When Erica dashed into the house, she realized that she had not gotten the groceries that she wanted to buy but she had no time to ponder that right now. She was talking to Caleb again and he said he loved her. *Love was a powerful thing,* she grinned to herself. With love she could overcome whatever problem he had been going through.

She skipped into the shower singing at the top of her voice, and with a big smile on her face. She was done with being afraid of Caleb's past. Whatever it was she would deal with it.

She was heading out of the shower and toweling off when she heard the phone ring. She hurried to get it.

"Hello, Erica," It was Lola and she sounded slightly mollified.

"Hi Mom," Erica said brightly. Her mother had been giving her the cold shoulder for the past two weeks and had rarely called.

"I am going to church tonight, so I can't stay and talk," Erica frantically dried her body.

"Well," Lola said hesitantly, "your father has something to tell you about that guy… I mean Caleb."

"Ooops," Erica said, "I had forgotten about that detective report… the guy took so long."

"It surprises me how blasé you are taking this man's past," Lola said and then huffed. "Anyway, your father has gotten all the details and…"

"Meet me at church," Erica said frantically, "I have to do the health lecture tonight."

"Okay then," Lola said. "I was planning to come to church anyway. Fred is actually ready so we'll see you there."

Erica hung up the phone and then found her pink dress; she always thought she looked extra pretty in it. Tonight she was going to meet Caleb and they would finally get to talk. She sprayed on her favorite scent, gave herself the once over in the mirror, and rushed out.

When she got to the church, the parking lot was unusually full for a Wednesday night. Usually the attendance was sparser but since the health lectures, more people were coming out.

She got out of the car hurriedly and entered the church lobby. Pastor Brick was talking to a group of people and he waved her over when she entered.

He turned to Erica. "They are having song service now. After that Sister Gena, will introduce you and then we'll have the testimonies and prayer section."

Erica nodded. "Okay, I will just give the technicians my jump drive with the presentation."

Pastor Brick nodded absently; he was already caught up in the conversation that was going on around him.

Erica couldn't wait to get the presentation over and done

with so that she could go and talk to Caleb. She wondered if he had arrived yet. She kept looking behind her to see if he was around. He arrived when she was in the middle of listing the different types of exercises that people could do from home. He sat in the back. She saw that he was dressed all in black and she stumbled a bit over the few words she still had to say. He looked masculine, and handsome.

The church was fairly packed with quite a few members and visitors. She tried to get back into the presentation but her eyes kept straying toward Caleb. He gave her a discreet thumbs up.

She grinned and continued with her presentation, finally breathing a sigh of relief when she finished—the question and answer session was relatively easy for her to handle. Phoebe wanted to know how she lost the weight; she told her that she engaged in a particularly taxing outdoor activity.

Her mother winced at that and Erica breathed a sigh of relief when she didn't get up and say something about it.

When she finished, she went to sit beside Phoebe who called her over but she wanted to join Caleb at the back.

"Your ex-con is here," Phoebe cackled softly when she sat beside her in the front.

"I know," Erica said, excited.

"So you found out what he was in for?" Phoebe asked curiously.

"No," Erica looked at her. "Frankly, I am going to trust my instincts where he is concerned and I am going to wait for him to tell me."

Phoebe shrugged. "I would want to know without delay. Suppose he's psychotic or a serial killer."

"Stop it," Erica whispered.

"Thank you, Sister Erica," Pastor Brick was saying from the front. "I think these health lectures can make a difference to the way we operate on a daily basis." He patted his paunch. "I will take into consideration some of those pointers you gave us.

"And now we will have our testimony time. Our first testimony will be from our infamous church visitor, Brother Caleb Wright. He has been visiting with us for close to seven months. He was actually baptized in prison. I don't want to take up too much of his time so I invite Brother Caleb to come forward."

Erica gasped. "Caleb. What's happening?"

Phoebe snickered beside her. "Well now…I guess we are about to find out."

Erica looked across at her mother.

Her mother had a serious look on her face and her father was smiling slightly.

Erica's heart picked up speed and she inhaled deeply, exhaling in spurts. She wondered if she could deal with his announcement publicly.

Well, she would have to because he was heading for the front; his slight bowleg giving him that extra sexy walk.

It was her turn to be supportive so when he picked up the mike she gave him a thumbs up and then tensed her spine in anticipation of his testimony.

Chapter Twenty-Three

Caleb headed for the front of the church. He had not realized how far the walk to the front was, and how many people were in church. They were all staring at him and when he turned around, he took a deep breath.

He had never been comfortable with crowds. He always preferred the hustle and bustle of a kitchen, and allowing his food to speak for itself rather than facing people en masse.

Now here he was, about to give his testimony. He had thought about it all of this evening and then he had come to church bold as you please and asked the pastor for the opportunity. He did it for two reasons. He didn't want the continuous whispers about his past to hamper his attendance at the church anymore and he wanted to put Erica's mind at ease. This was the best way to do it, he thought.

He cleared his throat. "Goodnight everyone." The church members eagerly told him good night. He could see the gleam of curiosity in their eyes and the nervous apprehension in Erica's.

"Well, as you may have heard, I was in prison for five years, four months, three days and two hours. I know the exact time because when you are in prison every single minute can be torturous. You track time and it moves so slowly.

"Before prison, I thought I was happy. I had a job I loved, I was married to a beautiful woman… she had a daughter from a previous relationship but I took the child for my own. I had a family, something I never had when growing up.

"Then my wife had an affair with a lawyer and decided that she didn't want me in the picture anymore. I had no idea that she was plotting to strip me of every material possession that I had bought to make our lives comfortable."

He coughed and then cleared his throat.

"I was a fairly decent fellow even then before I knew God. My wife would pick fights and I would walk her out and wait for her to calm down. Apparently, she wanted to spur me to violence but I was not that kind of person, so she became desperate." He paused.

Erica had her eyes closed tightly but Phoebe was whispering in her ears furiously.

"Well, she wanted me out of the way so badly that she decided that she would have me locked up on sex abuse charges. So my stepdaughter was coerced to report to the police that I had been sexually abusing her."

The church gasped and fierce whispers could be heard. He waited for them to quiet down.

He looked at Erica and saw tears in her eyes. He gulped. He had wanted to tell the bare bones of the story as emotionlessly as possible but Erica's tears were getting to him.

"So, I was picked up at work by the police, fingerprinted and herded into a cell with a bunch of criminals. The police said they had evidence. My stepdaughter was adamant that

I had touched her inappropriately for years and that I had threatened her if she told anyone. Her mother, my ex-wife, suddenly recalled times when I behaved in a violent manner, threatening both of them.

"I was assigned a lawyer to fight my case but my wife had meticulously planned my demise. She had emptied our joint account, prepared divorce papers and had found some legal loophole to strip me of ownership of our house.

"My family stopped visiting me—the few of them that I had. Even my father abandoned me. I was convinced that when I went to court to answer charges of sexual molestation of a minor that I would be exonerated...surely people could see the truth, I thought. The evidence was weak; they really had nothing to tie me to this so-called abuse, but my stepdaughter testified. She gave the performance of her life. Even to myself in that courtroom I sounded like a monster.

"The judge gave a swift and heartfelt sentence. She said she had no tolerance for people like me. I was so bewildered when I heard that I had gotten twenty years to life that my lawyer said I laughed.

"Let me tell you church," he cleared his throat. "It was rough the first two years in prison. I thought I would have lost my mind. I was innocent but everybody declares his or her innocence in prison. I was not alone in my pronouncement of innocence, but I knew, and God knew that I hadn't done anything wrong. Through those first bitter years, he was preparing me for greater blessings.

"A woman visited me in prison who told me that she was impressed to give me her Bible. It was one of those well-used Bibles from a woman who actually read it. It was marked-up with highlights that actually made it easy for me to follow related passages.

"I read the word, and one night I surrendered myself to

Christ. I said to him, if you can get me out of here I will be ever so grateful. I felt within myself that I had to let go of the bitterness that I was feeling toward my wife, by now she had divorced me and had moved on with her new life.

"I was baptized on a Sunday in the prison chapel and I helped my fellow cellmates to know of Jesus for themselves. I had totally left my fate up to Christ and had stopped hoping for a miracle.

"But one day the legal aide lawyer, who had represented me in court, showed up with a grin on his face. He said, 'Mr. Wright, your stepdaughter went to the police and confessed that she was coerced by her mother to accuse you and that you were a good father to her. She confessed the whole thing.'

"I was ecstatic, but it took two months for all the legalities to be sorted out so that I could be set free, by then my reputation was in the toilet. The court system apologized but those people who have no idea about my story will forever tarnish me with the moniker of being a child molester."

Several persons were shaking their heads in pity when they heard this.

"There is one thing that I don't regret about prison though," he said grinning slightly. "I got to know the Lord, and I learned that this world and its materialism, our busy lives, and our fixation on self are also a prison if we do not set aside time to focus on something bigger than us. I am happy that I got to know Jesus before it was too late."

Shouts of Amen could be heard at this statement.

He was about to put down the microphone when he hesitantly brought it up to his mouth again; his hand trembling slightly. "I swore off women for years and wanted nothing to do with them. Understandably, I had trust issues."

He heard chuckles coming from the congregation.

He turned and looked at Erica. Her eyes were shining brightly, a pleased smile on her lips.

"But then I met a woman who loved me for myself and I intend to keep her."

Erica gasped.

"Erica Thomas, will you marry me, I love you."

"Awww," the church gasped.

Erica couldn't believe it. He was actually proposing to her in front of the entire church. She got up. Her legs were trembling and her hands shaking. "You bet I will."

Loud claps were heard and then there was a standing ovation from the church brethren. Lola came to hug her daughter first and then gave her a squeeze. "That's what the investigator heard. I guess he said it all. You have our blessing."

Erica hugged her Mom.

Caleb reached her next, a smile on his face as he embraced her tightly. "My Erica."

"My Mr. Wright," she whispered. "I love you too."

THE END

Keep reading for an excerpt from **Unholy Matrimony**,
Phoebe's story

Phoebe sat in the front pew of the church for the wedding ceremony and tried to look pleasant. Erica had not let the dust settle under her feet after Caleb had proposed to her in front of everyone at church.

Her friend had gone into a mad flurry of excitement and had started planning her wedding the same night. She had declared that she wanted a church wedding at twilight on a Saturday and that she wanted the whole church to attend. No invitations were necessary and none was given. Erica had posted the date on the notice board and a cheekily written invitation to a reception after the service.

Phoebe looked behind her; the church was packed to the hilt. In a bid to make up for insinuations they made up against Caleb, the ladies of the church had outdone themselves with the decorations. Erica had requested a chocolate and burnt orange theme with hints of gold and they had gone all out, some of them even wearing the same colors to coordinate with the theme. Even Phoebe had made an effort to coordinate her outfit and had haggled over the gold dress she was wearing with a store clerk who was reserving it for 'that rich lady Hyacinth Donahue.'

Phoebe had almost had a fit to get it. Once more she was reminded why rich people were better off than the poor masses. She had finally gotten the dress and had counted it a bittersweet victory. Once again she had vowed that one day, they would all be chasing her to buy their merchandise and she would shun them. Oh, how she would shun them.

The junior orchestra was playing as Erica glided up the isle in her mother's lace dress—on her father's arm.

She looked beautiful and so pleased that, for once, Phoebe felt a glimmer of happiness for someone who had the audacity to tie the knot before her. Her happy feeling didn't last long though as Tanya leaned toward her and whispered, "isn't she gorgeous?"

Phoebe nodded but her mood changed and she was gripped by a sudden onset of depression. When would she ever find a man who loved her as much as Caleb loved Erica, or even as Pastor Theo loved Kelly?

Theo and Kelly were sitting at the end of the same pew she was in. Kelly was beaming, her hair was tied up in an elaborate chignon and she was dressed in a chocolate brown dress with a sprig of orange flower in the bodice—Theo was holding her hand as if they were newly weds.

Phoebe noticed that they had not carried the baby; only their two older children were sitting beside them.

She sighed and Tanya looked at her, her brows raised. "It's a wedding, cheer up."

"I know," Phoebe whispered, "but it's just that Erica and I discovered Caleb. If I hadn't driven him away that could have been me up there getting married and being happy."

Tanya chuckled. "He was poor at the time of your discovery, remember?"

Phoebe snorted, "but he's not poor now, is he?"

"No he is not, but the best part of all of this for him is that he has a woman who loves him, whether he is poor or not."

"What are you trying to say?" Phoebe whispered fiercely, "that I am a gold digger?"

Tanya mumbled, "who the cap fits...now shut up, they are about to say their vows."

Phoebe felt like strangling Tanya, but she valiantly tried to tune her mind into the service. Erica declared her 'I do's' loudly and with confidence and Caleb was handsome in his tuxedo and had a pleased smile on his face.

Pastor Brick, the attendant pastor declared, "wherefore they are no more twain, but one flesh. What therefore God hath joined together, let not man put asunder. I now declare you husband and wife. You may kiss your bride Mr. Wright."

The deed was done.

Phoebe watched as Caleb and Erica engaged in a deep kiss that had the congregation oohing and ahing.

Tanya looked at her and grinned. "Their honeymoon is going to be hot enough to burn."

"Shut up," Phoebe snapped.

"What's gotten into you?" Tanya's smile slipped, "usually you are more fun to hang out with. You know if you could only let go of your prejudices, you would find someone."

"Argh," Phoebe growled, then forced a smile on her face as the bride and groom turned to the congregation. "You don't know what you are talking about."

Tanya was clapping with the rest of the congregation and said to Phoebe sideways, "we'll pick this up in the church hall at the reception. Erica said she had more chocolate treats prepared than a chocolate shop."

Phoebe got up reluctantly when the usher indicated to her row first. She traipsed behind Tanya obediently and went to the door to congratulate Erica.

"Pheebs," Erica squealed when she saw her friend, "you wouldn't believe what Daddy and Mommy gave us as a wedding present?"

"What?" Phoebe asked injecting a note of excitement in her voice.

"We are going to Paris!" Erica squealed.

"Just for two weeks," Caleb said beside her.

"That's lovely!" Phoebe exclaimed, "I wish you all the best for the future... I am so happy for you."

Erica giggled. "Thank you my dear, I hope you find your Mr. Right soon."

Phoebe moved on as there a crush behind her to congratulate the effervescent bride. She walked out into the night air and spotted Tanya who was waving to her.

"As I was saying," Tanya said when she drew near, "you need to lower your expectations a little bit."

"Never," Phoebe said, a steely finality in her voice, "there must be a tall, dark, handsome, rich man in the world for me."

Tanya laughed. "There is. He's in your dreams, so dream on."

Phoebe looked over at the crowd with a sad feeling in the pit of her stomach. Maybe she really was aiming too high. Maybe she was too picky and unrealistic, but oh how sweet it would be to go for a honeymoon somewhere far away, without pinching pennies like Erica was.

"What about that guy Charles Black, your neighbor?" Tanya asked interestedly, intruding on her thoughts. "He is really good-looking."

"Poor," Phoebe snorted. "I don't even know what he does for a living."

Tanya giggled. "What about Ezekiel Hoppings? The rich ugly guy?"

"I gave him my number last week at church," Phoebe responded sullenly.

Tanya choked back a laugh and then erupted, "are you serious? Are you really serious? The beautiful Phoebe Bridge who will not tolerate imperfection in anyone gave her number to that unfortunate looking man."

Phoebe shuddered, "I did. He asked, 'is it okay for me to call you sometime?' I said yes. End of story. He hasn't called since and I didn't take his number. So there, that's the end of that."

Tanya shook her head in awe. "I am sorry I dared to lecture you Pheebs. If you can consider Ezekiel Hoppings as a date, no matter how rich he is, I can say your standards of perfection are well and truly lowered. Let's go and have some of those delectable chocolate desserts that the groom made. Erica has been harping on about them all week."

OTHER BOOKS BY BRENDA BARRETT

Love Triangle Series

Love Triangle: Three Sides To The Story- George, the husband, Marie, the wife and Karen-the mistress. They all get to tell their side of the story.

Love Triangle: After The End--Torn between two lovers. Colleen married her high school sweetheart, Isaiah, hoping that they would live happily ever after but life intruded and Isaiah disappeared at sea. She found work with the rich and handsome, Enrique Lopez, as a housekeeper and realized that she couldn't keep him at arms length...

Love Triangle: On The Rebound--For Better or Worse, Brandon vowed to stay with Ashley, but when worse got too much he moved out and met Nadine. For the first time in years he felt happy, but then Ashley remembered her wedding vows...

New Song Series

Going Solo (New Song Series-Book 1)- Carson Bell, had a lovely voice, a heart of gold, and was no slouch in the looks department. So why did Alice abandon him and their daughter? What did she want after ten years of silence?

Duet on Fire (New Song Series- Book 2)- Ian and Ruby had problems trying to conceive a child. If that wasn't enough, her ex-lover the current pastor of their church wants her back...

Tangled Chords (New Song Series- Book 3)- Xavier Bell, the poor, ugly duckling has made it rich and his looks have been incredibly improved too. Farrah Knight, hotel heiress had cruelly rejected him in the past but now she needed help. Could Xavier forgive and forget?

Broken Harmony(New Song Series-Book 4)- Aaron Lee, wanted the top job in his family company but he had a moral clause to consider just when Alka, his married ex-girlfriend walks back into his life.

A Past Refrain (New Song Series-Book 5)- Jayce had issues with forgetting Haley Greenwald even though he had a new woman in his life. Will he ever be able to shake his love for Haley?

Perfect Melody (New Song Series- Book 6)- Logan Moore had the perfect wife, Melody but his secretary Sabrina was hell bent on breaking up the family. Sabrina wanted Logan whatever the cost and she had a secret about Melody, that could shatter Melody's image to everyone.

The Bancroft Family Series

Homely Girl (The Bancrofts- Book 0) - April and Taj were opposites in so many ways. He was the cute, athletic boy that everybody wanted to be friends with. She was the overweight, shy, and withdrawn girl. Do April and Taj have a love that can last a lifetime? Or will time and separate paths rip them apart?

Saving Face (The Bancrofts- Book 1) - Mount Faith University drama begins with a dead president and several suspects including the president in waiting Ryan Bancroft.

Tattered Tiara (The Bancrofts- Book 2) - Micah Bancroft is targeted by femme fatale Deidra Durkheim. There are also several rape cases to be solved.

Private Dancer (The Bancrofts- Book 3) Adrian Bancroft was gutted when he returned to Jamaica and found out that his first and only love Cathy Taylor was a stripper and was literally owned by the menacing drug lord, Nanjo Jones.

Goodbye Lonely (The Bancrofts- Book 4) - Kylie Bancroft was shy and had to resort to going to confidence classes. How could she win the love of Gareth Beecher, her faculty adviser, a man with a jealous ex-wife in his past and a current mystery surrounding a hand found in his garden?

Practice Run (The Bancrofts Book 5) - Marcus Bancroft had many reasons to avoid Mount Faith but Deidra Durkheim was not one of them. Unfortunately, on one of his visits he was the victim of a deliberate hit and run.

Sense of Rumor (The Bancrofts- Book 6) - Arnella Bancroft was the wild, passionate Bancroft, the creative loner who didn't mind living dangerously; but when a terrible thing happened to her at her friend Tracy's party, it changed her. She found that courting rumors can be devastating and that only the truth could set her free.

A Younger Man (The Bancrofts- Book 7)- Pastor Vanley Bancroft loved Anita Parkinson despite their fifteen-year age gap, but Anita had a secret, one that she could not reveal to Vanley. To tell him would change his feelings toward her, or force him to give up the ministry that he loved so much.

Just To See Her (The Bancrofts- Book 8)- Jessica Bancroft had the opportunity to meet her fantasy guy Khaled, he was finally coming to Mount Faith but she had feelings for Clay Reid, a guy who had all the qualities she was looking for. Who would she choose and what about the weird fascination Khaled had for Clay?

The Three Rivers Series

Private Sins (Three Rivers Series-Book 1)- Kelly, the first lady at Three Rivers Church was pregnant for the first elder of her church. Could she keep the secret from her husband and pretend that all was well?

Loving Mr. Wright (Three Rivers Series- Book 2)- Erica saw one last opportunity to ditch her single life when Caleb Wright appeared in her town. He was perfect for her, but what was he hiding?

Unholy Matrimony (Three Rivers Series- Book 3) - Phoebe had a problem, she was poor and unhappy. Her solution to marry a rich man was derailed along the way with her feelings for Charles Black, the poor guy next door.

If It Ain't Broke (Three Rivers Series- Book 4)- Chris Donahue wanted a place in his child's life. Pinky Black just wanted his love. She also wanted him to forget his obsession with Kelly and love her. That shouldn't be so hard? Should it?

Contemporary Romance/Drama

The Preacher And The Prostitute - Prostitution and the clergy don't mix. Tell that to ex-prostitute, Maribel, who finds herself in love with the Pastor at her church. Can an ex-prostitute and a pastor have a future together?

New Beginnings - Inner city girl Geneva was offered an opportunity of a lifetime when she found out that her 'real' father was a very wealthy man. Her decision to live up-town meant that she had to leave Froggie, her 'ghetto don,' behind. She also found herself battling with her stepmother and battling her emotions for Justin, a suave up-towner.

Full Circle- After graduating from university, Diana wanted to return to Jamaica to find her siblings. What she didn't foresee was that she would meet Robert Cassidy and that both their pasts would be intertwined, and that disturbing questions would pop up about their parentage, just when they were getting close.

Historical Fiction/Romance

The Empty Hammock- Workaholic, Ana Mendez, fell asleep in a hammock and woke up in the year 1494. It was the time of the Tainos, a time when life seemed simpler, but Ana knew that all of that was about to change.

The Pull Of Freedom- Even in bondage the people, freshly arrived from Africa, considered themselves free. Led by Nanny and Cudjoe the slaves escaped the Simmonds' plantation and went in different directions to forge their destiny in the new country called Jamaica.

Jamaican Comedy (Material contains Jamaican dialect)

Di Taxi Ride And Other Stories- Di Taxi Ride and Other
Stories is a collection of twelve witty and fast paced short
stories. Each story tells of a unique slice of Jamaican life.

CPSIA information can be obtained at www.ICGtesting.com
Printed in the USA
LVOW10s2124240415

436067LV00001B/5/P